Turquoise
Summer

A NOVEL

Turquoise Summer

BY MARY BETH LAGERBORG

ISBN: 978-1-938633-42-3

Published by Retelling
RETELLING.NET

In cooperation with Samizdat Creative
SAMIZDATCREATIVE.COM

Cover design by Cynthia Young
YOUNGDESIGN.BIZ

Cover photo courtesy of the Grand Lake Area Historical Society
GRANDLAKEHISTORY.ORG

Cover images by DIGITALFARMER/ISTOCK + STILLFX/ISTOCK

For Adeline and Eleanor

And in memory of my grandparents, Arthur Jay Carruth, Jr.,
and Norma Hawley Carruth

Kitchen Conference

ON THE NIGHT before they left for Colorado, Maggie's grandparents' house didn't feel regular. The front hall was disturbed with a jumble of suitcases and boxes, and past Maggie's bedtime she heard voices in the kitchen. The eleven-year-old sleuth crept down the wide dark staircase and peered through the crack between the door frame and the closed swinging door to the kitchen.

Her grandparents sat on one side of the yellow Formica table, with their chairs nearly touching. Facing them across the table sat their maid Alma, her arms and elbows a forklift on the table for her sagging shoulders and bulging bosoms. Dark circles pooled across the smooth black skin under Alma's eyes. Obviously she was too tired for whatever they were talking about at this time of night. Maggie knew that under the table Alma's feet would be splayed free from her shoes, her bunions flaring.

Maggie had watched at this door before. In fact, she had watched life in her grandparents' home from many vantage points. From here, Maggie had watched Alma and her husband Baxter loosening at the kitchen table when he picked her up after work. They'd talk low and slow as Baxter ate the generous slice of apple pie or cushion of custard that Alma always saved from dinner for him.

Tonight a dark shape lingered on the outside of the kitchen door to the porch, a black cut-paper silhouette through the filmy lace curtains. Baxter must be waiting out there for Alma, like a dog kept on the porch because his paws were dirty. Sure enough, a slice of chocolate cake sat ready on the counter next to the sink.

"I know it's short notice," Nana was saying. Maggie's grandparents had been beauty-parlored and barbered for their vacation trip. Grandpa's ruffle of gray hair ringed his shiny head with the boundaries clipped and tight. Nana's silver-streaked dark brown page-boy hugged her ears in upside-down question marks, and Maggie smelled lingering permanent wave solution. Nana's mouth was stuck in her bridge-party smile. The two of them posed a counter-weight to the bulk of Alma. "You know we don't like to operate this way," Nana continued, "but now we have to take Maggie, and what are we supposed to do on a month's vacation with an 11-year-old—like Maggie?"

Maggie put her hand over her mouth, to clamp it shut.

"Besides, we'll have dinner parties, and Max will show up, and he makes such a mess," Nana said.

True, when her Uncle Max came home from college, he left clothes and dishes in the wrong places, making her grandparents' home look more like her own.

"We really did hope for a rest, Alma." Nana said, although Alma looked like the tired one.

Maggie watched Alma lean forward, as if they were playing cards at the table and it was her deal. Then Alma stuck her left hand into her uniform pocket where Maggie knew she kept her rabbit's foot, and paused some moments, as if reconsidering her play.

"Yes, Miz Hamilton, I hoped for some rest too," Alma replied. "You promised me this time, and Baxter took two weeks off. He's never taken two weeks off. I promised Mama we'd come spoil her awhile." Alma said this louder, as if for Baxter to hear.

"I'm sorry, Alma, but sometimes plans change, and we just can't

2

help it. I've waited through a damn war for this vacation, and I'm going fishing!" Grandpa pounded his fist on the table, like he did every time he talked about the "damn war."

"I'm not planning on taking Mrs. Hamilton's guests on tours or babysitting on the stream. We don't get on very well without you, you know, Alma," Grandpa summed up, his mouth looking down and toady, but his eyes gentling on Alma.

Now Alma folded her arms, which were big like Popeye's, and leaned back. She pursed her lips together, then folded her lower lip over her upper lip and sucked on that a while. "Where would I be stayin'?" she asked.

"Actually, Alma, you'd have your own cabin in back of the main house. It's a nice bedroom / sitting room and a bathroom with a shower." Nana said.

Alma whistled softly through her teeth and rolled her eyes around one circuit. A train whistle moaned and Alma glanced toward Baxter on the porch. He stood sideways and rigid, as though listening.

The kitchen windows were open, the one behind Alma to the backyard, and the one over the sink to the screened-in porch where Baxter waited. No breeze softened the heat of the August Kansas night. The kitchen was as hot as the outside, so how would a breeze know which way to move?

Alma reached over to a pile of used table linens on the counter, shook a napkin from the pile, and mopped perspiration from her forehead. Feet shuffled on the porch.

Nana rapped her polished fingernails on the table. It was not good to keep Nana waiting. The question sat there like the cumquats in the fruit bowl at the center of the table—Would Alma come? Maggie was confused. Could Alma tell her grandparents "no"? Maggie couldn't. Could Alma?

Grandpa removed his round wire-rimmed glasses and rubbed the purple indentations where the glasses seated along the bridge of his hooked nose, as if Alma's stalling was a painful nuisance, like his glasses.

3

"You know we wouldn't ask you to change your plans unless it was an emergency," Nana said, shortly, like she was talking to the furnace repairman.

"What is the big house like?" Alma asked. Grandpa sighed and rose to take the slice of chocolate cake from the counter. He stood leaning against the counter and ate it.

"The cabin is old, but in some ways it's simpler to keep up," Nana said. Grandpa paused and raised his eyebrows, posing a silent question over a bite of cake, but she shook her head at him.

"Are there mountain lions?"

"Rhaaaaa!" Grandpa roared. Alma and Nana looked at him, startled. Maggie cupped over a giggle.

"Nay," he said. "No mountain lions. But the name of the cabin, Kawuneeche, is an Indian word for coyotes. Now coyote, on the other hand—"

"Oh, Frank," Nana said, swiping a hand at him. "Stop."

"What would I do different there?" Alma asked.

"The only difference is that you'll have to watch Maggie most days, in addition to the housework. I know she means well, but you just never know what she will do if she has free rein. Her poor pregnant mother is exhausted from trying to keep her occupied, but also keep her close in case she needs her."

Alma squirmed on her seat, then asked, "Miz Hamilton, would you say I'll have some free time?"

"Time? You'll work basically the same hours, Alma. Sundays off and Thursday evenings. Just like here."

"But . . . you being on vacation and all, will there be days with some l-a-t-i-t-u-d-e?" Alma spread out her hands, stretching out time between them.

Nana scowled. Grandpa, who was scraping the last bit of chocolate frosting from the plate with his finger.

"Well, perhaps some time here and there could be arranged, but you'd have to . . ."

4

"—We just don't do very well without you, Alma," Grandpa repeated, nodding at both women.

Maggie pushed the door, which opened with a pop, and stood in the kitchen in her baby doll pajamas. She straightened her glasses, under the ledges where rubber bands had held pigtails in her shoulder-length auburn hair.

"I have an idea," said Maggie. "I could stay in the maid's cabin, and Alma could stay in my room. She would be closer to the kitchen, and I wouldn't disturb anyone."

"Of course you can't stay alone out there, Maggie," Nana said. "Now please go back to bed. You shouldn't be lurking about." Maggie hated Nana's interpretation of her investigative talents as "lurking." Monsters and murderers lurked—not Maggie.

"Miss Maggie, the big cabin is more likely haunted than the little one. You'd best stay there," Alma said softly. She motioned with her nose for Maggie to leave, which she did. Nana closed the swinging door and stood in front of it. The voices became muffled and softer. Chairs slid against the floor, and Maggie ran up the staircase.

Baxter fumed as they walked to the car. "No way do you have to do this, Alma. How come you didn't just tell them 'no'?"

Alma drew up close to Baxter and shushed him with a finger on her lips. She motioned to a point of light out on the lawn that was not a lightning bug, but the end of a cigar. "Mr. Hamilton," she whispered.

Baxter backed his 1944 blue Plymouth down the driveway, entered the street and jerked the car into gear. In a half block he turned right and sped down the dark street with the car windows open.

"I took time off for you, Alma. What am I s'posed to do with you gone?"

"You can do whatever you can't do cuz you're always travelin'," Alma said.

"I don't understand you. They don't own you," Baxter said. "You don't have to go. So what if they fire you. I can support you."

Alma studied the passing houses. "It's not the money," she said. "And no, they don't own me." *And you don't neither*, she thought.

"I know I'm gone a lot, Alma, but train porter's best job there is. I thought takin' two weeks off would make you happy."

"I'm grateful, Baxter, you know I am. I know it wasn't easy gettin' off. But they need me."

"And I don't?" Baxter looked at her, incredulous. "I get one piece of your coconut pies, Alma, and they get the rest. Always." The muscles tightened on his right arm, extended over the steering wheel. "Ha! And tonight I got nothin'." He looked straight ahead. Baxter's hair, barber-trimmed weekly to look sharp under his uniform hat, was sprouting some gray. His features, just good side of ordinary, had begun settling along creases.

His gray hair reminded Alma that at thirty-nine, she was ten years younger than he was. His work kept him gone more than at home, and so he did just fine without her. And, of course, they didn't have a child to worry about.

"You know, Baxter, maybe I'd like to see some other places too. You ever thought of that? Maybe I'd like to see how life happens someplace else. I haven't been on a train once in my life, 'cept for the time you brought me from my Mama's house, and our honeymoon weekend in Kansas City. That's it."

"Well, why didn't you never come with me?" asked Baxter.

"Cuz I'm always workin'—or have you noticed that?"

"Why you bein' sharp with me, Baby, and so soft with the white folk in there?" Baxter watched for a reaction, which she didn't give him.

"You can still go see Mama. She'd like that. You can help her out, and she'll cook for you." Alma tried to build a vacation scaffolding for Baxter without her. "You could do some fishing. How long's it been since you've been fishing?"

"Oh, yeah, Baby. Givin' me a little l-a-t-i-t-u-d-e," Baxter mocked.

Alma didn't reply, just watched the houses pass; at some, folks lingered on the front porches. She hugged her insides tight. Didn't matter what Baxter thought. Alma had a chance to make the most of her circumstances. To add some seasoning to the pot of her life, and give it a good stir. For just one month. If nothing else, she could see if life was different in a cool mountain place. Maybe people there would treat her with some respect.

Sitting in bed, Maggie opened to the first chapter of *The Mystery of the Crumbling Wall*, one of two new Nancy Drew mysteries that she was bringing with her on vacation.

She heard the rumble of Baxter's car, and went to the bedroom window to watch Alma and Baxter drive off. Since being trundled off to her grandparents' house today, Maggie's summer felt unhinged, and she didn't know where to put in the screws. Unrest was disturbing for someone who believed herself the double of the unflappable Nancy Drew.

If anyone needed Alma's help, Maggie thought, it was her mother, not her grandmother. If Alma could come help Maggie's mother, if her father would just accept Alma's help, then Maggie could stay home and play with her friends outside all day, instead of being tethered inside where her mother, sprawled on the living room davenport with a mixing bowl by her head, "might need her." Her mother had miscarried twice since Maggie was born, and her doctor said she needed bed rest. At their house this was davenport rest, because it was close to the window air conditioner. Her Nana was meddling to offer Alma's help. That's why her father said Alma couldn't come work at their house.

At least Maggie was now free from her mother's beck and call. And maybe the unhinged-ness she felt would be what was needed to propel her into her first full-fledged mystery. Who knew what might be ahead of her in an old cabin on a wild mountain lake? Maggie imagined the possible mysteries—

The Message of Echo Mountain
The Sign of the Dry Fly
The Clue in the Creaky Cabin
The Mystery of the Missing Grandmother

Alma was coming along. No matter how bad Nana's attitude was toward Maggie, she counted on the buffer of Alma. The Big Buffer. Maggie giggled.

Maggie remembered a passage about Hannah Gruen's unquestioning loyalty to Nancy Drew:

The kindly woman cared for the motherless girl as lovingly as if she were her own daughter, and worried a great deal whenever she thought harm might befall her.

A housekeeper like Hannah Gruen stilled the waters of everyday life so that Nancy Drew could eat well; sleep snuggly; recover from automobile chases in inclement weather; receive timely communications by telegram, post or telephone; and entertain clients befittingly. A month was a long time, but in a dark, creaky cabin, with Alma as her Hannah Gruen, Maggie was sure she could find and solve her very first mystery.

Maggie doubted that Alma had any idea what a crucial role she had to play this summer, and she wished that she could explain this to Alma, to make her feel better. She should have told Alma that she was the final piece that completed the picture in the jigsaw puzzle of her summer. If Alma came . . . If Alma would just come, what could possibly go wrong?

Through Kansas

FRANK HAMILTON WHISTLED softly as he navigated his new 1947 Oldsmobile on a two-lane highway through Kansas in the middle of an August night. His elbow rested out the open window; his shirt-sleeve flapped in the wind.

Frank had named his car the Gray Gazelle. As it leapt across the indistinguishable miles, he was wide awake with the excitement of a dream fulfilling.

Editor of the *Topeka State Gazette*, Frank was a happy fugitive from his desk, fleeing the dog days of summer in a city he knew too well, where too many people who knew too much wanted attention from him. Through the grinding sadness and stress of World War II, he had kept his paper reporting as honestly and faithfully to the facts as he could.

Now, after four brutal years, Frank headed toward their cabin, for a month of fly-fishing with his mountain neighbor and mentor, whom he called the Professor because of his willingness to instruct on all things related to dry flies and fishing. Day after fishing day on the streams would culminate with a boat ride, a Scotch, then dinner of pan-fried trout. Frank would sit by the fire and read or play cards at night. At his leisure, he would type his weekly column to mail home, the part of his job he loved most. Frank's life seemed so full he felt guilty. Peace at last; his family safe. His son Max had just missed conscription with the war winding down, so he'd been out of harm's way.

The headlight beams caught tumbleweeds, conventions of insects, and an occasional ambling farm truck. Heat lightning worried the western sky, and the two-tone gray Olds with its torpedo back sliced through the night at 70 miles per hour.

They traveled at night, to avoid the searing heat of a Kansas highway in late summer. Frank's wife Jane slept in the passenger seat beside him, her head resting against her dainty travel pillow. He glanced in the rearview mirror to verify that his granddaughter Maggie was also sleeping, with her head propped on a cosmetic case and her feet sticking out the window. In the other quadrant of the backseat, Alma rocked along, fanning herself with a magazine and watching the lightning. *Alma's a woman strong enough to stare down a storm*, Frank thought. *We'll see what she can do with Maggie.*

Frank chuckled, remembering the past Saturday. Maggie came over on Saturday mornings, walked across the street for her piano lesson, and then returned for lunch with them before they took her home.

Frank should have considered, before he pulled the cord from the trap door in the upstairs hallway ceiling and lowered the retractable wooden stairs to the attic, that he would be discovered. But he and Jane had lived alone for so long that he had lost all sense of caution.

The air in the attic was so old and unstirred that Frank had to remind himself to breathe. His head, shoulders, and then his body ascended the wooden stairs into a large room, opening upwards to the peaked roof joists, with windows at the two ends and storage shelves along the walls. Dust cloaked each article: each suitcase and hatbox and footlocker, each neglected instrument and book.

He walked to the shelves nearest the east window. Swiping the dust with his handkerchief, he coaxed from slumber the fishing tackle he'd stored for too long: wading boots, his favorite sweat-ringed felt hat, his leather pocketed vest, a wicker creel, a slicker, goose grease to treat his lines, a reel, and his bamboo fly rod standing upright in its metal case in the corner. Each of these friends—simple, efficient, clean although weathered—was more than ready for the trip.

Frank was proud of his paraphernalia, many pieces selected under the tutelage of the Professor years ago. As a final preparatory gesture, Frank opened his fly box and stroked his collection of Doctor Litsinger's, Professor Hoffstots, and furry blue Ed Arnolds, each dry fly named for a fishing companion whom he would join in a few days. Where they would fish was a question this year because of a water reclamation project, but not whether they would fish. Every day, if Frank had his way.

Looking through the attic window into the tops of wind-tossed trees, Frank imagined that he could hear running brooks. He paused from his packing tasks, sucked air from the room's thick heat, and re-united the three lengths of his fly rod. His fingers embraced the cork grip. As he stood in the center of the room, he experimented gingerly and discovered that the roof was high enough that he could arch the rod up, back behind him, and then snap it forward with no impediment. He grew bolder and swished a dozen strokes or more until sweat ran down his face and his grip on the rod slackened. With each cast he flung responsibilities off the tip of his line. No insufferable cocktail parties. No political wranglings. No daily oversight of the cover story. He attained a soothing rhythm, out and back and out the line circled.

Frank snapped the rod forward and nearly catapulted himself to the floor for fear of striking his granddaughter, who appeared at the top of the attic stairs.

"Grandpa," Maggie asked, hands on her hips, "why are you fishing in the attic?"

* * *

Now, with his fishing gear safely stowed in the trunk of the Gray Gazelle, Frank chuckled again. He passed a dark farmhouse, with its barn and rusty equipment huddled within a circle of trees for protection from the prairie-scorching sun and continuous wind. This time when he looked in the rearview mirror, Maggie returned his gaze. This child had an uncanny ability to startle him. Perhaps it was those eyes. She had her mother's eyes, and yet Adele's seemed focused and clear, while Maggie's eyes kept you wondering: Were they green or gray? Or green with gray around the edges? Her glasses magnified them, teasing him to decide: gray or green?

"What are you laughing at, Grandpa?" Maggie asked. He smiled, but didn't answer.

Maggie retrieved her glasses from the crease in the backseat and put them on to see if she'd missed anything. But they traveled a ribbon of road that stretched without end through fields of ripening wheat.

Unaccustomed to being up in the wee hours, Maggie considered the experience. Out the car window her extended hand dove buoyantly through the waves of hot wind. She watched the heat lightning, anticipating its flashes. Maggie wondered if these night hours were worth less than the daylight and evening hours, because people weren't up doing things in them. Did they even pass faster than the other hours? But then she remembered that night hours in Kansas were probably day hours in China, so that all hours got their just due someplace.

Maggie hadn't packed any dolls in the trunk for this vacation, although some of her friends still played with them. No, with Maggie it was all about real life—the intelligent, competent, invincible, golden-haired Nancy Drew.

The wind whipped the loose hair from Maggie's pigtails and drew all the moisture from her face. As a Kansan, she was used to this sauna-like wind, and it whispered adventure as the car sped along in the middle of the night.

Nancy Drew, eighteen and attractive, sped down the road in her yellow convertible. The young sleuth felt a rush of excitement as she raced toward her destination, that just might hold the solution to a mystery.

Maggie assessed her situation. Her parents had sent her away for a month with two old people—one who was over-particular and another who fished in the attic—a stuck-on-himself college-boy uncle, and a colored maid. Each of these people was all right sometimes, but when you put them together . . . for a month?

Still, home was no fun for Maggie. Her mother didn't even fix her peanut butter sandwiches, and her daddy worked too hard to give her much time. And he yelled in his sleep, which was enough to spook anybody, and it stamped a heaviness in Maggie's heart. She hoped he would be done with this by the time she got back.

Maggie was certain a big mystery awaited her. Didn't many of ND's mysteries take her on sailboats or motorboats that she piloted on rivers and lakes? She knew she would solve a mystery, and everyone would be so proud of her.

"Just like Nancy Drew."

"No, she's even better. Even brighter."

She would donate her reward to local orphans, and her grandpa would write her up in his newspaper column. Her parents would encourage her sleuthing once she became famous, and Nana would marvel at how clever and well-mannered she was.

In the front seat, Nana roused, peeled her shoulder from the damp upholstery, put her pillow in her lap and sat upright, staring into the night. She ran a brush through her matted pageboy and adjusted the combs that held the hair back off her face on either side. Maggie wanted to think of the women in her family as beautiful, leaving room for her own certain development, but the word she heard associated with her Nana was "handsome," which was a more hard-edged word. As she studied her grandparents' profiles in the dark, Maggie recognized to her dismay that the prominence of both their noses was a strong strike against her.

"Wakeeny?" Nana read the passing highway sign.

Grandpa looked at her with raised eyebrows. She gazed at him evenly, but eventually with a slight concaving at the dimple on the left side of her face. He reached over and squeezed her knee. She slapped his hand away, but she was smiling.

"Excited?" Grandpa asked.

"Yes," Nana nodded. "Happy to be getting away. Hoping it will be as wonderful as I remember. I'm not sure what 'vacation' means to me now, though. Especially with . . . " Nana nodded her head toward Maggie in the backseat, but of course Maggie was tracking with the conversation, so Nana might as well have said her name.

"But I thought bringing Alma was supposed to make the difference for you," Grandpa said.

"Hmmm. Yes, I know. But I guess I don't know what 'difference' looks like. What is it that I even want to do? It's fine for you, because you have your fishing, and the column."

"Well, you have your knitting, Janie. And bridge club will snatch you up as soon as they know you're there. Your reading and crosswords. You don't want to be *busy* do you?"

"It's about passion, I suppose. I want to love doing something, like you do." Nana pulled her compact from her pocketbook and powdered her nose using the little mirror. "Something of substance," she said as she snapped it shut. "Something fresh and new and promising."

She shifted in her seat to face Grandpa. "Say Frank, what if you let me write the Willows on vacation?" Nana asked. Grandpa had named his weekly column "Under the Whispering Willow" for his favorite weeping willow tree out in a Kansas field.

"It's just four issues," she said, as Grandpa began to protest. "You said 'maybe.'"

"Well, we'll see." Grandpa tried to pinch her knee again, but she caught his hand mid-air.

Maggie studied Alma, who wore a blue plaid shirtwaist dress and sensible new-looking black shoes, but she'd taken them off, and her feet rested on top of them.

"I feel sorry for Baxter," Maggie said to Alma. "Couldn't he come too?"

Still watching out the window, Alma tucked in her lips, as though considering.

"Oh, Maggie, that would hardly have been a vacation for Alma. And what would Baxter do?" Nana answered, without being asked.

"But I didn't think Alma was coming to be on vacation. I thought she was working," Maggie protested. "I bet Baxter likes fishing. He could go fishing with Grandpa."

"Maggie, stop. It's too late at night," Nana said, waving a hand at her. Alma turned a warm eye to Maggie and chuckled softly to herself.

A sequence of small billboards loomed on the horizon. "Hey, Maggs, here they come," Grandpa said.

"Don't stick," Maggie read the first sign in the headlights.

"Your elbow," Grandpa took the second.

"Out so far," read Maggie.

"It might go home"

"In another car."

"Burma Shave!" they shouted.

After they passed Limon, Colorado, the heat lightning dissolved, and they watched for the first sighting of peaks on the horizon. Maggie called out when she saw them, a dark mass against the lighter, star-brightened sky, as if cut jaggedly from a sheet of black construction paper.

As they approached Denver, with the wind in the car windows finally cool against their skin, they sat forward, enthralled by the lights of the city rising from the plain with the black hulk of mountains as a backdrop.

"Denver!" exclaimed Nana. "Diamond stickpin in the bosom

of the West." This was the most disgusting expression Maggie had ever heard, because it included her most hated "B" word. But she kept her mouth shut so she wouldn't have to discuss it. To Maggie, Denver meant cowboys and Indians and mountains—and mystery.

3

Taking Up Residence

ALMA WALKED THE INCLINE to the main house early on the first morning, picking her way over rocks and pine needles. She paused and stood tall, gathering in deep breaths of the light air. "Smells like Christmas," she said, smiling at the pine trees, shaking her head, and walking on.

She wore her powder blue zip-up-the-front uniform, this being Monday. Each weekday she wore a different color uniform, saving her white and her black taffeta trimmed in lace uniforms for serving at parties. Against a morning nip in the air, she'd tossed a pink cashmere sweater around her shoulders, from a sweater set that Miz Hamilton got for her at the Next-to-New. Her hair was pinned up under a kerchief.

On her first look-through of the cabin the day before, Alma had found much to her particular liking, but that could not redeem the fact that a monster resided in her kitchen. A monster that had been fed and harbored for many, many, many a year until she, unsuspecting, had been hoodwinked into his territory. She must tame him quickly, before he even thought he could mess with her considerable reputation.

She chose to first ignore him, walking from the screened back porch through the kitchen, through the dining room, and into the front screened-in porch, a soothing destination from which she could collect strength for battle. The porch was fixed out to be a comfortable place to stare at the lake by the hour. Wicker chairs on either side of a daybed all faced the lake. The daybed was fluffed and warmed by a row of red pillows and a multi-color striped knit afghan.

Outside the screens, fog obscured the mountains across the lake nearly down to the water line, like white window shades drawn down not quite to the sill. A strip of dark pines peeped through between the fog and the water, a swatch of green that widened as the fog gradually lifted. The pine trees, close-packed together, were mirrored in detail in the still waters of the lake. With mountains surrounding the water, Alma felt like she was in a deep bowl of beauty. Like a glass marble in the bottom of a crystal bowl, she could roll around inside it, but it would not let her go. It felt both wild and safe.

Alma felt Maggie's presence and glanced over as Maggie climbed onto the daybed and tucked her feet under her, wrapping up in the afghan. They watched the fog gently swirl and rise without the need to talk.

"Glory," whispered Alma.

"Nana's up," Maggie observed, as she caught sight of her grand-mother sitting in a swing on the dock in a jacket and headscarf. Nana sat still except for a gentle swinging when she pushed against the dock with her foot in a house slipper.

"Um hum," said Alma. "Who said the two of you's could be up so early?" Alma set a hard eye on Maggie.

"Why can't we be up?"

"I was hopin' in the mornings I could have a spell by myself to get the coffee on and get a sense of the day."

"Like you own the place," Maggie taunted, and Alma just smiled. *Yes, ma'am*, she thought.

"You been here before?" Alma asked.

"When I was little. But it's like I remember it."

"My whole life's been in Kansas," Alma said. "Even my honeymoon was jazz and barbecue in Kansas City. And this is *not* Kansas."

"Ugly old Kansas."

"No," Alma sighed. "You just haven't lived there long enough to appreciate it. But it's shore not like this."

Alma left Maggie on the daybed and retraced her steps through the dining room and into the kitchen to set straight who'd be the boss. The clanking of metal on metal that ensued sounded like the bowels of the house had indigestion, and Alma feared she'd wake Mr. Hamilton. Maggie came to the kitchen and found Alma stuffing kindling into the front of a red and white enamel wood stove.

"Go there to the wood box on the back porch and fetch me some kindling," Alma instructed. Maggie brought an armload of twigs and helped Alma load the chamber, then watched her take a long kitchen match from the holder on the wall, strike it on the top of an iron burner lid, and tickle the flame against the twigs until they caught.

"How'd you know how to do that?" Maggie asked.

"By watchin' my Mama," Alma replied. "Back in the Dark Ages."

Alma straightened, put her hands on her hips and said, "Miz Hamilton didn't tell me nothin' 'bout this beast. I shore hope your grandparents don't expect to enjoy my usual level of cookin' now that the ruuules have been changed."

Alma gave Maggie a tour of the various black openings in the top and front of the stove. On the stovetop the four burners were iron disks, each with a notch cut into them. They could be removed by an iron handle stuck into the notch. Maggie lifted the front right disk with the iron handle and peered inside the hole. Then she seated the lid back down with a clatter. On the stove front there was a left chamber for the wood fire, a rusty compartment on the right for boiling water, and a center chamber for baking.

"How do you know how hot each part is getting?" Maggie asked.

"Just what I was wondering myself," said Alma, banging the iron handle on the stovetop.

Alma's experimentation soon led to a coffeepot rhythmically bubbling on the stove. She intended sizzling bacon and fried eggs for breakfast, but after three attempts kept company in the garbage on the back porch, she served up boiled eggs, toast, and cornflakes instead. When Nana appeared in the kitchen the fuming and the sighs coming from Alma warded off any criticism that she may have been fixing to make.

"We'll have fried eggs and bacon tomorrow mornin', Miz Hamilton," Alma said. "I'll be getting' up crack o' dawn to do it," she muttered into the soap bubbles at the sink. Nana just ignored that.

After breakfast, Grandpa's fishing friend, whom he called The Professor, but Nana called Edgar, bumped along the cabin's rutted gravel driveway in his old black Ford. Grandpa waited for him with his rod, dressed so that all of his tackle gee-gaws dangled off him.

"That there hat makes Mr. Hamilton look like a man hangin' out on the Woolworth's corner downtown," said Alma as Maggie helped her clear off the table.

"But the bandana 'round his neck is jaunty," said Maggie.

"Bring me trout for dinner, and I'll figure how to cook 'em," Alma called after him. He waggled his hand in reply.

Before lunchtime, Alma settled into a cleaning routine that would breathe life into a long-shuttered place. She opened all the windows and dusted room by room, from walls to lamps to furniture. She moved along as sprightly as she could, so homesickness couldn't catch up with her, but it came snapping at her heels.

At lunchtime she was ready for a break. A quick survey out the screened porch told Alma that Maggie had met neighbor children, so she prepared accordingly.

Alma carried down to the lake a plate of pimiento cheese sandwiches, a bowl of potato chips, and five Coca-Cola bottles balanced in the center of a red wooden tray. She sashayed along, placing both feet on one step before moving to the next. It was hard to see the next step over the tray, so her dance was slow.

She set down the tray on the table in the center of a log gazebo near the beach, where Miz Hamilton sat knitting. The three children swarmed over, wrapped in their beach towels.

"Thank you, Hannah," Maggie said as she grabbed a Coke, which she wedged between her knobby knees to pull off the cap with a bottle opener from the tray. Alma put her hands on her hips and squinted at Maggie.

"Now Miss Maggie," Alma said, "have you forgotten that I go by Alma when I'm in Colorado?" She stared at Maggie without her usual hint of a smile.

"Oh yes, silly me!" Maggie tilted up her soda to take a swig, and grinned around the bottle at Alma.

"And who are your friends?" Alma asked.

"Yes, Maggie," Nana called from the gazebo, with a hint of irritation, "please introduce your friends."

"Tell them who you are," Maggie waved her hand at the girl and smaller boy standing beside her.

"I'm Jamie Gerrard, and this is my little brother Benjamin, but we call him Bebo." Jamie said politely. Even with her wet hair stringy down her back, Jamie was blonde and becoming lovely. She had long legs and the beginning of curves. Obviously she was a couple of years older than Maggie, who was thick through the center and whose swimsuit mostly sagged at the top.

"Oh yes, you must be John and Norma's children," Nana said.

"Yes ma'am," said Jamie.

"And are they both here?"

"My mother is, but my father's in medical school in Denver. He comes up when he can."

"I heard he saved many lives in the war. I'm sure you're very proud of your father," said Nana.

"Yes, ma'am," the children replied. Bebo's smile had blank spots where teeth were missing.

"Well, please help yourself to lunch, which Maggie should have offered to you before she started," Nana said. "Would you like a Coke?"

The children spread their beach towels on the grass and sat cross-legged, soon blowing foghorn sounds in the tops of their bottles.

Nana and Alma sat in the gazebo chewing their sandwiches and staring out at the lake, which was shimmering in sunlight and dabbled with color, like a water color painting: flags on poles, beach toys, motorboats towing water skiers, sailboats.

On her lap Nana spread the soft bulk of the yellow blanket she was knitting for her daughter's baby. Alma stretched out her legs, fanned her face with a napkin, and silently watched Miz Hamilton knit, enjoying the easy informality of eating with her employer in a gazebo on a beach—a scene as totally foreign to her as would be her cooking in the White House for the Trumans. More so, even, since in that case she'd be in a kitchen—with an electric stove.

The forming blanket was soft, with perfect, even stitches. Alma had worked for this woman long enough to know that this was a problem: Miz Hamilton's life was worked in even rows and perfect stitches. But her husband, and her children, and especially her granddaughter, dropped stitches now and again. Alma also figured that perfection could get boring after fifty-eight years.

As she worked, Nana glanced up when the wind rose or a boat passed or a child laughed. "I've dreamed of this on winter nights in Kansas," she said presently.

"I see why you like it," Alma said, feet out-stretched, and hands clasped in her lap. "It's the most beautiful place I've ever seen," said Alma. "But it's wild, too."

"Wild?"

"The edges are civilized, almost too pretty," Alma said slowly, thinking it through. "The rim part is civilized, with houses and boat garages. But you don't know what's down deep in all that water. And the forests up above are dark and closed."

Nana paused her needles and gazed at the lake. She had a strong, slightly large nose with a ledge at the top, but taut lips that were never without lipstick. And dimples when she smiled; Alma thought the dimples were her best feature.

"The way the mountains surround the lake, you wonder if it's like an ice cream cone and the lake bottom goes down way deep," Alma formed a pointed-bottom cone with her hands.

Miz Hamilton peered above her reading glasses at Alma and showed her dimples. She kept stitching.

"Sometimes the beauty hurts," Miz Hamilton said presently.

"Like heart-burn?" Alma asked, drinking her Coca-Cola.

Miz Hamilton laughed so heartily that Maggie looked up from their game of Crazy Eights on the beach.

"Alma, I want to *do* something!" Miz Hamilton confided. "I want to *love* to do something, like Frank loves his fishing. It's not so much his preoccupation with fishing that bothers me; it's that I don't have a fishing. Did I ever love doing anything like that? If I did, I've forgotten."

"I know just what you mean, Miz Hamilton. I've been feelin' that way too. Or like I just want to try something that I didn't even know I could do." Even as the words spilled out, Alma wanted to wipe them up. Fool! Why should she share thoughts she held closely with her employer?

"Alma, what on earth would you do?" Miz Hamilton tugged out a long length of yellow yarn. She said it like a statement, not a question, and Alma let the matter fall to silence. She listened to the little waves lapping the shore.

"Maybe I'll try fishing too—but in my own way," Miz Hamilton continued. I could go out on the lake in the outboard and enjoy watching the activity on the shore while I troll. I could come in if I got bored or had an engagement in the afternoon or if the weather turned nasty. I could even go through the channel and fish on the new reservoir. What do you think?"

Alma wiped the corners of her mouth for any errant pimiento

cheese. She looked at Miz Hamilton's linen pedal pushers and white blouse, and her matching Keds. Alma was not impressed. What should she say? This did not sound to her like the right pursuit for Miz Hamilton.

"You'll have to watch Maggie while I'm out in the boat," Miz Hamilton continued. *And what was so different about that*, Alma wondered.

"And you'd have to help me clean the fish. At least at first."

"You might consider taking Miss Maggie with you, at least a time or two," Alma ventured.

"I'm not so sure that I want to spend slow days on the lake with Maggie," Miz Hamilton said. "Nor she with me."

"Well, that boat is a little small for the two of you, but if you're looking for a little spark in your life—"

"Maggie thinks I'm a mean grandmother. Mostly, I think, because I'm so worried about her mother. I don't want Maggie to wear her out or distress her. At her age, Maggie ought to know some manners. And I think this whole Nancy Drew thing just aggravates her more annoying qualities."

"Have you read one, Miz Hamilton?"

"Well," she stammered, "why would I read Nancy Drew?" She scowled and her needles clicked, and the soft spell in the gazebo passed.

The kids had spread their beach towels on the dock in the shade against the boathouse, and played Crazy Eights.

"Where are your parents?" Jamie asked.

"At home. In Kansas."

"Why aren't they here?" asked Bebo.

"Because my mother is trying to have a baby," said Maggie. Jamie giggled, but Maggie ignored her. "They knew I would be bored at home, but if I came here my summer would be rich in opportunity."

"Opportunity for what?" Bebo asked. He slipped in a card that wasn't the right number or suit, so Maggie picked it up and handed it back to him.

"For solving mysteries," said Maggie. "That's what I do best."

"Clubs," said Jamie, and discarded an eight. "Like what mysteries have you solved?"

"Like the mystery of the stolen diary key. The mystery of the dead parakeet. To name a few." Maggie slapped down the four of clubs.

"Well, I've read Nancy Drew too, you know," said Jamie. "And like calling your maid 'Hannah'—that's ca-ra-zy." Jamie played the eight of hearts.

"No it's not. Alma is very much like Hannah Gruen. She cares for me like I was a motherless child, as lovingly as if I were her own, and she worries a great deal whenever she thinks harm might befall me."

"Oh, brother! First of all, Hannah Gruen is not colored."

"Is too," said Maggie.

"Is not. I'm sure she's not."

"Well, show me if you're so sure," said Maggie. "Which ones have you read, anyway?"

"Lots. *The Secret of the Old Clock. The Secret of Shadow Ranch. The Clue of the Broken Locket. The*—"

"How about *The Clue in the Crumbling Wall*?" asked Maggie. Or *The Mystery of the Tolling Bell*? I brought them with me. I can loan them to you when I'm finished."

"We'll see. I'd rather draw and paint. And ride horses."

"We can ride horseback then," said Maggie. "What level of rider are you, beginner or intermediate?"

"I have my own horse at home, Maggie, so I'm advanced."

"Well I don't have a horse, but I'm advanced too," Maggie replied, as Jamie shifted position with a sigh. The card game was flagging.

"Do you want to have a baby brother or a baby sister?" asked Bebo.

"No," said Maggie, matter-of-factly. She could feel Jamie scowling at her.

"Are there any mysteries around here?" asked Bebo, who played the wrong suit or number as if he didn't care any more.

"I wanted to ask you that, since you've been here for the summer," said Maggie. "Have you heard anything suspicious?"

"Well, there's a haunted hotel," Bebo pointed to a slip of land that jutted into the lake.

"How is it haunted?" Maggie put her cards face down on the beach towel and looked where Bebo pointed.

"'Some men were killed there in the cowboy and Indian days."

"But none more recently?"

"Not that I know of," Bebo said.

"I'll ask my grandpa about that tonight. I'm trying to persuade him to be more of a Carson Drew and encourage me with his bright mind and knowledge of everything going on, and give me some notoriety in the newspaper. Until I can persuade him, I'm handicapped. Except that I do have a Hannah Gruen!"

Jamie threw in all her cards. "I'm tired of this. Let's go home, Bebo."

"Come on!" coaxed Maggie. "Don't you want to go to the haunted hotel? We could go on horses." She shielded her eyes and looked up at them. Jamie grabbed up their beach towels, making the cards fly, some into the water.

"I was hoping you can help me solve mysteries," Maggie said, "if your services prove helpful."

"Well, aren't we la-ti-da," said Jamie. "We may need to charge for our services—if they prove helpful."

"If we solve a big one, I don't see any reason why we couldn't split the reward, after we've taken care of any needy orphans and widows. Are you going to draw and paint all day, or are you going to have an adventure that will be of value to mankind?"

"Sheesh. Come on, Bebo." Jamie strode down the path to their cabin without looking back.

Mystery Found

GRANDPA WAS RIGHT about bridge club. As soon as Norma Gerrard learned that her children had been playing with Maggie, and that the Hamiltons had brought their maid, Jane Hamilton found herself not only a fourth for bridge, but the hostess.

The first day of bridge club was socked-in rainy, and Alma grumbled as she built a fire in the living room fireplace per Miz Hamilton's instructions.

"Is this or isn't this August, Miz Hamilton?" Alma asked her as she tossed in a log. "This climate's got my compass off."

Nana and Alma conferred in the kitchen over the hors d'oeuvres for the gathering, which they had decided would be Alma's Cheese Puffs. But Alma wasn't at all confident of the outcome.

"I've made Cheese Puffs 'nough times to constipate a cow—so crisp yet so delicate," Alma told Miz Hamilton, fluttering a hand, "but that's because I got the oven timing just right. And that is exactly what in a wood stove? If I peek to see if they're ready, they're goin' to fall." Alma leaned back against the sink and fingered her rabbit's foot in her white uniform pocket. She was emitting little bursts of air through her lips as if letting off steam so she wouldn't erupt.

"Well, just do your best, Alma. I'm sure they will be fine," Nana said.

Nana was tidying up in the living room, and setting out coasters when Maggie appeared wearing a gold leather fringed jacket.

"Maggie, where did you find that?" Nana asked.

"In the closet under the stairs. Can I wear it? It pretty much fits me, and it wouldn't fit you."

"That belonged to your great-grandmother, Maggie," Nana said. Maggie scooped her fingers through the fringe, as if waiting for the point. "You can wear it if you're very careful. And not in the rain. Ever." The jacket suited Maggie, Nana noted in surprise. It made her look older, and stylish.

"Thanks, Nana." Maggie smiled at her.

Nana had assigned Maggie to be Alma's helper for the afternoon, which of course was one of Nana's premier methods of teaching Maggie manners. When they entertained in Topeka and Maggie was there, Nana had her play a piece on the piano for the guests. This rarely went well, but was the price you paid for developing a child's talent, and their guests were indulgent.

Voices at the front porch door signaled that Nana's friends had arrived. After Nana's second call for Maggie to join her and meet her friends, Maggie went in to smile and greet Mrs. Louise Haggerty, a skinny old lady with a cane; Tilly Wyatt, a short-haired out-doorsy-type lady who seemed to bring the outside in; and Jamie and Bebo's mother Norma Gerrard, who had blonde hair like Jamie's and a nice small nose. Maggie said hellos and excused herself to help Alma in the kitchen.

A few bridge hands into the game, Nana's lips went taut as Alma lowered a platter of cheese puffs to the corner of the bridge table. Her palms raised, Alma fled to the kitchen, her rump rising and falling in her white uniform, before Nana could comment on the poufs of cheese and meringues puddled pitifully on their toast rounds. Nana remained silent to see how her guests would respond. Sometimes things were not quite as bad as they appeared.

She overheard Alma offering Maggie the extra cheese puffs in the kitchen. "No thanks," said Maggie. "You got any popcorn?"

"Why don't you go to the porch until I need you and read that mystery about the wall crumbling?" Alma whispered—not softly enough.

"How can I read when old ladies talk so loud?" Maggie asked, also too loudly. She zoomed through the living room and landed on the porch daybed.

Nana glanced at her guests, who studied their bridge hands.

"Well," said Nana, to settle in some conversation, "What do you all do up here?"

Three pairs of eyes looked at her quizzically, as if she'd posed a difficult riddle.

"I mean, what is it you look forward to here? How do you spend your time?"

"Oh, well, I love to go rowing on a calm morning," said Tilly gaily. "And hiking when I can find some companions, and pressing wildflowers. Occasionally I still do some sailing, when the men are desperate for crew," she laughed. The others tittered with her.

"Actually, I don't tell many people this, but I do some oil painting. I've dabbled for years. Took classes when I was young," said Norma. "But Jamie is interested in painting now, and it's quite a nuisance for me to try, because she also wants to paint."

"What was the question, dear?" asked Mrs. Haggerty, pawing to lift a cheese puff from the platter with her curled fingers.

"What do you like to do here at the lake?" repeated Nana, more loudly.

"Well I don't know about the rest of you, but I like to play bridge!" she said, as if to terminate the chit chat.

"What do you do, Jane?" asked Tilly a few hands later.

"I'm just trying to decide, frankly," said Nana. "We've just arrived and all. I thought I might take up fishing. And then Frank may turn over his weekly column to me for the duration," she said lightly.

"But isn't fishing a bit boring, Jane?" asked Tilly. "Never could see what the men find in it. But if you want to, of course."

"Why, Jane, I didn't know you were a journalist too," said Norma.

Nana was sorry she raised the question. What did they know about either fishing or writing columns? She felt protective against their smothering her tentative flames.

"Will Max be here for the Regatta?" Tilly asked Nana.

"Yes, he's coming up. He's working on the newspaper this summer, and Frank can only spare him for a couple of weeks. I'm not sure whether he'll sail in the races. The boat's been stored for so long."

"Our Jeffrey is looking for competitors. His father's given him a brand new E-scow. Says the cost is nothing compared with having Jeff home safe from the war in the Pacific." The women exclaimed that this was marvelous.

"Is Max writing?" Norma asked, "taking after his father?"

"No, actually he's a photographer."

"You mean local news stories? Automobile ads? He wasn't a war photographer . . . no . . . he wasn't, was he?" Tilly asked.

"Max didn't turn eighteen until the war was ending, Tilly. I'm sure you remember that he's a good four or five years younger than your Jeffrey."

"Yes . . . How very fortunate for him," Norma declared. "And what a blessing for you, Tilley, to have Jeffrey returned to you in one piece."

"How is John getting along?" Nana asked Norma.

"He adapts. He's like a man driven, finishing medical school. Says he saw so much worse overseas than what happened to him," Norma replied. The women muttered that this was so true.

After a lull, Nana said. "I'm sorry, girls. Alma's a bit off her game up here. The altitude and all. Apparently she hasn't cooked on a wood stove before. I guess it's beneath her." The women tittered.

"It's all right, Jane," said Tilly. "We would have had nuts and bridge mix at my house."

"But then you don't have a maid," remarked Louise Haggerty, who did have a maid, while she discarded.

"Alma," Nana called, her voice rising at the end, as if Alma were a child suspected of a prank.

Alma smoothed her apron and approached the bridge table. "Yes, Miz. Hamilton?"

"Do we have some bridge mix? Or some nuts?" Nana raised her eyebrows hopefully, in high umbrellas.

"Yes ma'am, I believe we have somethin' like that. I will certainly go check."

Moments later, Nana caught movement out the dining room window and saw Alma holding an umbrella and with a tablecloth wrapped around her shoulders trotting to her cabin out back in pouring rain. "Oh, my," Nana muttered, "where on earth . . . Maggie, would go see if you can help Alma? But put on a slicker so you don't get rain on that jacket!"

But before Maggie could find a slicker, Alma trotted back into the kitchen, and Maggie joined her.

Loud whispering slipped from the kitchen: "Haven't you got any bridge mix?" Maggie asked.

"Nope."

"But didn't you buy this candy yourself?"

"Yes, but I've got to do somethin'. I for shore do not want to leave your grandmother in an embarrassing position."

In her rush to bring a candy dish to the bridge table, Alma did not take off her shoes, and they squished liquid across the wood floor and left imprints on the Navajo rugs. Nana was distracted with the tracking as Alma placed her stash of saltwater taffy on the bridge table.

"Would you like a refill of iced tea or perhaps a Coca-Cola?" Alma asked politely as she removed the cheese puff platter, which remained half full.

"I'm sorry, girls," said Nana, when Alma left. "She is really so capable. But this is her first time in the mountains."

"Tell her to come visit my Coralee," said Mrs. Haggerty, who was seventy-eight, thin and sallow, and sat curved over into a "C."

"I don't know what I'd do without Coralee," she continued. "Now that Walter has passed away, the cabin is so dark and lonely, and I've been agitated this week."

"Why Louise, what's wrong?" asked pretty Norma Gerrard.

"I can't seem to find my squash blossom necklace," Mrs. Haggerty said. "It was a gift from Walter, and is very special to me. I only wear it here in the summer—it's so heavy on my neck, you know—so I leave it in the cabin, in a secret place where I keep a few valuables, but it's not there. I've searched high and low."

Suddenly Maggie stood close to Mrs. Haggerty's elbow, and the women unconsciously breasted their cards, for fear Maggie was watching their hands. Mrs. Haggerty hadn't thought to hide her cards, but since her hands shook with a palsy, it would have been hard for Maggie to make them out anyway.

"You say you've lost a valuable necklace?" Maggie asked Mrs. Haggerty.

"Well, yes, dear."

"When was the last time you wore it?" Maggie asked, fingering her jacket fringe.

Mrs. Haggerty squinted and put a long boney finger to her lips, as if it would help her think, but no answer came out, so Maggie continued.

"Did anyone borrow it—like maybe one of the bridge ladies who doesn't have one?"

The ladies chuckled and looked at one another—the look that women share when they assume they're all thinking the same thing— except for Nana, who was on the verge of turtle-eye, where her lids go two-thirds shut, to shield her eyes from what they have just seen her granddaughter do.

"Do you have reason to believe foul play, Mrs. Haggerty?" Maggie persisted.

"Maggie!" huffed Nana, "Where are your manners?"

"I'm sure I can't think so," replied Mrs. Haggerty, her frail frame shaking.

"Does anyone else know about your secret hiding place?"

"Only Coralee—and if I can't trust Coralee, then who can I trust?" Mrs. Haggerty laughed a tight, prissy laugh, looking around at her friends.

"Marguerite, that's enough!" said Nana. "I'm so sorry, Louise. She does need a little taking in hand. It's this steady diet of Nancy Drew mysteries. We were hoping that this summer. . . ."

"Nana, I just want to help. I really do," Maggie's foot stomped. It stomped again, dancing the fringe on her leather jacket.

"Thank you, Maggie," said Mrs. Haggerty softly. "I appreciate your concern. But I fear I've misplaced my necklace. Heaven knows it wouldn't be the first time," and the women all laughed drily.

"Would you let me know, Mrs. Haggerty, if you need help locating it? And especially if you find evidence that someone has broken in?" Maggie looked at her earnestly through her glasses. "I can search your secret place for you. If you need someone who can crawl. . . ."

"Maggie!" Alma called from the kitchen doorway, the call rumbling from her throat in a way that subdued the fireplace flame and made five females crane their necks. "Maggie, you come quickly now and help me with these beverages, you hear?"

"Just one more thing, Mrs. Haggerty." Maggie gathered her box of crayons and a sheet of newsprint from the desk in the corner of the living room and put them in front of Mrs. Haggerty on the bridge table. Nana rose and took hold of Maggie's shoulders to guide her.

"Excuse me, Nana. Just a minute," Maggie said.

"Could you please draw a picture of the necklace, so I would know if I found it."

Mrs. Haggerty took up the crayon box as if this sounded like fun. She deliberated which color to pick, and finally pulled out the silver, but her slender, gnarled fingers seemed unsure how to grasp it.

Nana pulled the paper and crayons gently from her friend and handed them back to Maggie, turning her and motioning for her to take them away.

Mrs. Haggerty looked up. "It's a squash blossom, dear," she explained. "Heavy matrix, quite green. You know." She lifted a finger as if to jog Maggie's memory as to exactly what she meant.

Alma appeared to refill the ladies' glasses. She caught Maggie's eye and motioned her to the kitchen. Maggie took the paper and crayons with her, pausing in the living room to pull the dictionary from the bookshelf.

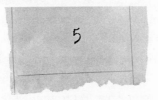

5

Sunset Cruise

AT FIVE O'CLOCK that evening, Grandpa revved the Chris Craft
motor to resurrect his tradition of a sunset cruise. The lake had
metamorphosed from slate gray during mid-day rains, to choppy
waves and sun in the late afternoon, and now to an evening stillness
that brought boaters out for a circuit of the lake at the peaceful close
of a summer's day. To Maggie's delight, since Nana said she needed
a nap before dinner, Grandpa and Maggie would cruise alone.

Maggie sat in the front passenger seat of the sleek mahogany craft
that had two cushioned bench seats separated by a large wooden box
housing the motor. If Nana had come along, Maggie would have
perched on top of the motor box, where a beauty queen would sit.
But the front seat also felt honored.

As Grandpa pumped the throttle back and forth, the boat furi-
ously cleared its throat. He pumped once more—to show off, Maggie
could tell. Then he eased it out of the boathouse and turned the boat,
named Adele after Maggie's mother, to cruise along the shore.

The boat felt so grand that Maggie pretended that Grandpa was
the king and she was the princess, surveying their kingdom by boat to
see if all was well. As the boat sliced through the calm green waters,

the motor gurgled gently. Maggie studied each cabin, wondering what its people were like, and what they were doing inside. Why weren't they out by the lake on a summer's evening? What had they done that day? The happiest houses were the active ones with tree swings and rowboats, jumbles of nautical paraphernalia, adults sitting on the dock and kids playing along the shore. Maggie and Grandpa waved when they passed people, whether they knew them or not. *Our adoring subjects*, thought Maggie. If Grandpa knew the people, he turned off the motor a few feet from their dock and called out, "How are ya? Catch any fish today? Bob up yet? Beautiful evening." Sometimes they passed a rowboat or motorboat and waved sedately.

At the lonely houses Maggie saw no signs of life through the windows or in the yards. Often they were particularly big houses that seemed sad and very probably haunted.

"Did you catch lots of fish today, Grandpa?" Maggie asked, feeling the need to converse like a grown-up in the front seat.

He sighed. "Nothin' that I didn't throw back. My heart wasn't in it."

"Why not?"

"Well, I'm grieving an old friend, Maggie. An old fishing spot that was like a good friend to me."

"Oh?"

"Used to be the Professor and I fished on the Colorado River, on a stretch that wandered through meadows thick with wildflowers: shrubs of yellow cinquefoil, white Indian paintbrush and my favorite, the scarlet gilia, like little red trumpets. But I'll show you what it looks like now. . . ." Grandpa steered the boat toward a narrow channel.

He eased the Chris Craft under the bridge with just inches to spare on either side. As they passed through into the channel, he urged Maggie to watch over her side of the boat, as he watched over his, to spot rocks and be sure they stayed in the water deep enough for passage. In about the length of a football field they passed under a second bridge and out into a lake that was larger than Grand Lake, but without houses or boathouses around it. Maggie checked over the side again and recoiled in horror. Just below the surface of the water waved creepy long grasses, bent on ensnaring them.

Grandpa idled the motor. "We won't go far in," he said. "New reservoir, Maggie. And soon this one will be connected to an even larger one at the far end of it."

"Why is it full of grass?" Maggie asked.

"Because they flooded fields and meadows. Sunlight still gets down to the bottom and makes the weeds and grass grow."

Maggie had never been on a body of water this large, and she found it unsettling, partly because theirs was the only boat in sight.

"My favorite fishing spot was about three-quarters down the lake," Grandpa pointed.

"Why'd they make this?"

"To irrigate crops in eastern Colorado, where it's drier than in Kansas. Part of each summer, they'll pump the water backwards, so it flows from these big reservoirs through Grand Lake, then through a tunnel under the mountains to Estes Park, and then on to the eastern plains."

"Whoa," said Maggie. "How'd they do *that*?"

"Over lots of years." They sat in the gently rocking boat, viewing acre upon acre of water.

"But now where do you fish?" Maggie asked as Grandpa turned the boat back toward the channel and Grand Lake.

"We'll find new streams," he said. "There're plenty up here. As much as I knew this change was coming, the reality is a shock. Change is hard when you get as old as I am, Maggie. After the war I was hoping this was one place where things were still like they used to be."

Maggie rode along giving her quiet as a comfort to her grandpa.

"Change is good too, I s'pose. Sometimes we try it on and it fits and we walk around in it. Other times the buttons holes don't stretch and the sleeves are too short." Maggie wrinkled up her nose and laughed at him.

As they passed out of the channel and resumed their circuit of Grand Lake, Maggie watched for the names on the cabins, which she figured gave clues about their owners: Sunshine Cottage, Lupine Ridge, Sky Rock, Pine Eyre, and Faraway. She made up names for the unnamed houses, giving dark names to the lonely ones: Musty Mansion, Lament Ledge, Secluded Stoney Way.

Most of the boats they passed also had names on their sterns, whether they were sailboats or motorboats: Suzanne, Marguerite—like her name!, Highball, Lady of the Lake, The Nana, Collette.

"I hear you uncovered a mystery today." Grandpa's eyebrows rose again. She liked it when he didn't wear a hat so she could see the full workings of his frolicking eyebrows.

"Grandpa, do you know what a squash blossom necklace is?"

"Isn't it a big old silver and turquoise necklace with an upside-down horseshoe at the center?"

"If you owned one of those, but it was missing and I could help you find it, wouldn't you be glad for my help?"

"Absolutely," said Grandpa. "Of course it would be important how you went about it. Reporters must be professional in how they investigate a story. Detectives too."

"What do you mean?"

Grandpa smiled at Maggie, and the blub blub blub of the slowly moving craft carried them in a companionable cradle.

"Let's compare it with the old codger brown trout I was thinking about today, Maggie. Back in the summers when I fished on the Colorado, I always found him in the same place—a lip of ground that pouted out over the river, where the willows overhung the bank, dropping choice insects for him to eat. We did battle many summers, the old codger and I, but I always put him back when I caught him. We had an agreement; we respected each other."

"Maybe I should have kept him one of those times we battled," he said, waving his hand back at the reservoir. "But what I mean is, you have to be careful how you address old codgers like Louise Haggerty.

And like your grandmother for that matter," Grandpa said, tugging on the nearest of Maggie's pigtails. "But don't tell her I said so."

Maggie thought about how Nancy Drew carefully broke the news to an ailing Mrs. Fenimore that her daughter Joan had been quite naughty.

"Never lose your honesty, Maggie," said Grandpa. "But you'll discover more clues with a little finesse."

"—speaking of, I'm hoping you can help me with a project. I think your grandmother needs something fun to do. Something she will thoroughly enjoy. If you have some ideas as to what that might be, I think that it would help us all." Grandpa winked at her.

"Sure, Grandpa," Maggie winked her left eye, then her right one because the other hadn't worked well. She was confident that she could help even Nana have a little fun.

Grandpa idled the boat while he pointed out a landmark to Maggie, a configuration of mountain peaks that the locals called The Lady of the Lake. If you looked at her green heights from just the right angle, the soft peaks formed the forehead, nose, and chin of a lady lying on her back. The ridges of the mountain adjoining The Lady of the Lake's forehead formed her flowing tresses. The mountain next after her chin, the rounded Mt. Baldy, was her . . . was her . . . Fortunately Grandpa didn't point this out to Maggie, using her most hated "B" word, but she silently observed it for herself.

When they reached the east shore, where the houses were farther between, Grandpa nudged the throttle. The boat's big motor responded, giving them all the speed they wanted as they sliced a curve through the water, kicking up a high double tail of spray. As they swept along the shore toward home, the sun set in salmon and gold.

While Grandpa idled the Chris toward its slip in the boathouse, beginning the maneuver several yards out, Maggie saw the Professor standing outside the cabin porch door, talking with Nana.

"I hope dinner goes all right," Maggie sighed. "Nana was pretty mad at me today."

"The Professor has an axe to grind with me too," Grandpa said.

"But he's your best fishing friend," Maggie protested.

"Yes, but there's something he wants me to do for him that doesn't fit my vacation plans."

"Finesse it, Grandpa!" Maggie said, resting her hand on his hairy arm.

As Maggie and Grandpa approached the porch, the Professor went inside. Nana met them at the door, and Maggie heard her ask Grandpa in a raspy whisper, "Do you suppose he'll drop in at dinnertime every night?"

Maggie needn't have worried that Nana would rehash the day over dinner, because she and the Professor, alias Edgar, bantered back and forth the whole time, teasing and contradicting each other.

After they had eaten the last crumbs of their generous slices of brown sugar pound cake, which was sunken in the center but tasted just fine, the Professor fumbled in his pockets for his pipe and matches, and Nana shooed the men outdoors to The Woodpile, a circle of low log benches near the stack of firewood. The benches circled a fire pit and served as grandstand seats for horseshoes. While the adults sat on the benches and talked, Maggie practiced tossing horseshoes back and forth at the pins. Grandpa started a fire in the pit. Nana wore her red wool jacket around her shoulders, and she pulled it close together in the front against the evening chill.

"Will you pitch horseshoes with me, Grandpa?" Maggie asked.

"Not tonight, Maggsy," said Grandpa, "but we'll have lots of nights to pitch shoes."

Maggie knew that's what adults said and maybe there would be, but probably there wouldn't. But to be fair, Carson Drew was always off on a business trip and didn't play with Nancy. Hannah Gruen wouldn't have tossed shoes with her either. Maggie needed chums, that's all there was to it. Maybe Jamie and Bebo would work. Didn't look good now, but it was too soon to tell.

The Professor lit his pipe and Grandpa chewed on a cigar. For awhile, as darkness embraced the mountains and the lake, the only sounds were from Maggie's tosses, generally thuds as the metal shoe hit the dirt short of the pin and cartwheeled into the grass. Lights twinkled from the inhabited cabins around the lake.

"The whole place seems changed in the four years we've been gone," said Grandpa. "More bars and hamburger joints in town. More people from the construction work on the tunnel and the reservoirs."

"Those things don't bother me," said the Professor. "Makes us sound like old snorts to complain about progress."

In the growing dark only the bulk of the Professor was visible, and smoke wafting from his pipe. Old Snort. Maggie pictured the name. "What bothers me is the way the Bureau of Reclamation's project's been done, with no regard for protecting the clarity of the water of Grand Lake," he said.

"Yes, I know," said Grandpa, "but all those clippings you sent me, from *The Denver Post* and *The Rocky Mountain News*, underlined in thick pencil . . . You seem to think that just because I'm a newspaperman I have the power to spank the federal bureaucrats and make the projects go away."

The Professor was a snorter, and Grandpa was a spanker. Maggie giggled in the dark.

"The power of the press, Frank. You've always touted the power of the press."

"Sure I do. The belief's type-set into me. But the Colorado-Big Thompson Project is a big boy's battle that's been waged over decades in Washington and Colorado. What do you think I can do from my desk in Topeka?"

In the darkness Maggie identified her first ringer by the clank of metal on metal. The adults clapped for her. The red glow of the tip of Grandpa's cigar marked where the adults were huddled in the dark.

"There is something you can do here, Frank, if you're willing to

41

give the town a little help with your time and your typewriter, to help us articulate our concerns to the Bureau. Also you can also forward our cause in your columns."

"But it's done; you can't make this go away!" Grandpa protested.

"I know that. We just want them to make good on their promise to keep the waters in Grand Lake clear like they were."

"My columns print in Kansas." Grandpa said, poking at the fire with a stick so that sparks popped and scattered. "And besides, I came here to fish. I need a vacation as much as the next fella."

"Kansans come here too, Frank," Nana said quietly. "Look at us! They come to enjoy the natural beauty. They come to fish. We could split it up. I could write the columns for you, and you could help on Edgar's town committee."

And Nana is a moocher, Maggie decided, stringing it with snorter and spanker. She hoped Grandpa was smart enough to see how Nana was moving in on his columns, for which Grandpa was famous at home. She knew this because people at the grocery store commented to her about them.

"I don't know, Janie," Grandpa said, tossing his stick into the fire and burning an end to the conversation.

6

Modeling at Thunderbird's

ONE TALENT THAT Maggie had developed to perfection, and that contributed immensely to her sleuthing, was the ability to slip up on people undetected. She mastered her craft at home, where her mother wanted nothing so desperately as quiet for her naps. Maggie's mother complained that even the whir of the window fan kept her awake. In the opportune afternoon hours when her mother was sleeping, Maggie had learned to be silently active in order to do what she wanted to do.

On this morning, Maggie crept down the stairs and into the kitchen hoping to snatch a couple of Alma's gingersnaps to munch in bed while she wrote in her diary. She stopped abruptly at the doorway to the kitchen, flattened herself against the outside of the open swinging door, and peeked around it. Alma sat at the kitchen table with her back toward Maggie, her bottom engulfing the round metal kitchen chair like it was no more than a bicycle seat. Maggie listened, scarcely breathing, as little bursts of air, like staccato whistles, emerged from Alma's lips.

Alma was examining what looked like a piece of stationery, tapping it with a pencil. She crossed something off, then wrote a word, and, as if on second thought, wrote another one. Then she doodled and drew around the edges. Alma wore her yellow uniform, so it must be Wednesday, and had pulled Grandpa's red and black plaid fishing jacket around her shoulders.

Coffee bubbled companionably on the wood stove, and Maggie decided that she would join her, that nothing important kept Alma from wanting company. Besides, Maggie wanted to get a good look at that piece of paper.

"Good morning, Miss Maggie!"

Maggie bent to be enveloped in Alma's hug, then pulled up a chair beside her. "What are you doing?" Maggie whispered. She didn't want to waken anyone and have to share her.

Alma held a sheet of stationery from the Olin Hotel in Denver, where the Hamiltons had stayed a night on their way to the mountains. Centered on the sheet in Nana's elegant handwriting it said,

WEDNESDAY, AUGUST 6TH
BREAKFAST AT 8:00 A.M.
SAUSAGE LINKS AND SCRAMBLED EGGS
ORANGE JUICE, CINNAMON TOAST, AND COFFEE
FRANK FISHING—PACK SANDWICHES BY 9:00 A.M.
VACUUM
PICNIC LUNCH ON BEACH: DEVILED HAM SANDWICHES
DINNER FOR 4 ON PORCH AT 6:30 P.M.
CURRIED CHICKEN* AND RICE
GREEN BEANS ALMONDINE
LEMON MERINGUE PIE WITH CHERRY TOPPING

"Five years I've worked for your grandmother," said Alma. "Five years of mornings she's written out the menu and the day's work for me."

Maggie could see that Alma had penciled in the drawing of the stately hotel at the top of the stationery.

"Your grandmother means well," Alma continued. "She's hoping to contain the day by setting it out on the page. But life spills off the borders onto the table." Alma held the paper by its top, and waved it back and forth as if it was wet. "And I bring the tea towel to mop up the spills." Alma grinned so that her eyes crinkled and her teeth gleamed like sunshine.

Maggie wondered how old Alma was, and looked for tell-tale clues. Her skin was smooth and shiny, without wrinkles except where her smile fanned out in tiny cracks along her eyes. When Alma was with Maggie's grandparents, she seemed young. When Alma was with Maggie and her new chums, she seemed old.

"Do you like doing that?" Maggie asked. "Wiping up messes?"

"Shore I do!" said Alma. "It's messy, but it's mine." Her teeth gleamed in a wide smile.

Alma leaned over to the stove, grasped the iron burner lid handle and rapped the stovetop twice. This was an action she'd adopted to assert her authority. Maggie shushed her. "You'll wake up somebody!"

Alma continued working on the stationery. In the top right corner she sketched Grandpa the Fisherman, his vest do-dads covering a round belly, a fish tail hanging out of his creel, a misshapen fedora on his head and a cigar in his mouth. Maggie giggled as Alma drew—amazingly well.

Alma moved her pencil across the menu. To the right of Curried Chicken*, Alma wrote "PAN FRIED TROUT?" Then she drew curling ribbons from the asterisk.

"Why'd you do that?"

"Anytime your grandmother uses this star, it means I'm supposed to get the recipe from *The Joy of Cooking*, which she thinks is like the *Holy Bible*." Alma wrote JOY JOY JOY, the words skipping along under the drawing of the Olin Hotel. She topped the hotel roof with a jaunty cherry.

"Your grandmother has no idea that her mother's lemon meringue pie recipe, that she thinks I follow by the letter, is actually the best in all of Topeka because I add soft bread crumbs to the lemon filling. Uh, huh! And oh, by the way, the fried chicken that Mr. Hamilton's important friends come back to the kitchen searching for, to

in shelves above the chairs and shoe-fitter stools. Up the center aisle, gift items enticed women like Nana to do their Christmas shopping at Thunderbird's in the summer time: linen hand towels with flickering hummingbirds, brass ashtrays shaped like sombreros with a crease in the top to hold a lighted cigarette, and serving platters painted with sprigs of pine branches.

Maggie led Alma down an aisle with Indian dolls in buckskin dresses whose black eyes closed when you laid them down, cowboy boots and hats, beaded Indian belts, and cap guns and rifles. She paused in front of a magnifying glass that swiveled out of a round metal case, and since it cost 49 cents, and she had plenty of money for that, she stepped to the front of the store to pry the coins out of her zippered coin purse and pay for it. Then she rounded up Alma from the postcard carousel and they got down to business at the jewelry counter in the back of the store.

A sales woman with wire-rimmed glasses in a navy blue dress watched Maggie and Alma approach. She was lumpy, with her grey hair in a wavy tight hairdo, and she reminded Maggie of her schoolteacher, who was referred to as an Old Maid. Like the card game.

The sales lady folded her white hankie—not lacy, just a plain one like Grandpa's—into the cuff of her short sleeve and placed her hands on the glass counter.

"May I help you?" she asked, pleasantly enough, but she looked like she was guarding a fort.

"We're looking for a squashed blossom necklace," said Maggie.

The woman looked Maggie and Alma up and down, and down and up.

"I believe you mean a *squash* blossom."

"Well, do you have one?" Maggie asked, palms up.

The woman smacked down onto the counter a fake black velvet "throat," and flipped through a key ring for the correct tiny key to open the display case. She clasped onto the velvet display neck the hugest piece of jewelry that Maggie had ever seen. A long double strand of round silver beads was interspersed with turquoise stones, each in an oval silver setting that flared out like a silver trumpet along the sides of the necklace. In the center, a six-inch-wide upside-down silver horseshoe held several turquoise stones, with the largest in the upper center.

Maggie whistled softly between her teeth and ran her finger over the surfaces. Then she pulled her new magnifying glass from her blue jeans pocket and studied the necklace thoroughly. She tried this with her glasses on and with them off, to get the best effect, which was with them off. "Each stone looks different than the others," said Maggie, wondering if the necklace was of inferior quality, although it was the most impressive jewelry she had ever seen up close.

"Yes," said the sales clerk. "Exceptional matrix. It's an heirloom piece. Navajo."

"Hmmm. Yes," said Maggie.

"Did the store buy this from someone here in town?" she asked.

"Mrs. Burton buys most of her jewelry on the reservations," the sales clerk sniffed, and withdrew her hankie to dab stray droplets from her nose. "She personally chooses our jewelry from the artisans. Each season we sell a few pieces on consignment for summer residents."

"They're pawned," Alma translated.

"I see," said Maggie, who could feel herself blushing with excitement. "So this could be from a local person."

"Yes, I suppose."

Alma nudged Maggie in the ribs. "Ask her to check her records," Alma said.

"I was just getting to that!" Maggie scolded. "Could you please check to see who this piece belongs to?"

"Well, miss, I cannot divulge that information, but I can tell you that the initials on the tag are CLN."

"Not exactly Louise Haggerty, unless the L is there as code in the middle," Maggie observed.

"Why is it called a squash blossom?" Maggie knew sometimes it was best to reveal your ignorance in order to learn something that would keep you from looking stupider later.

"Because the silver and turquoise settings along the sides represent the flower of the squash plant, which is a symbol of fertility," she said. "Squash, corn, and beans were the staple crops of the Pueblo, or farming Indians."

Maggie was sure this woman was related to her schoolteacher.

"The squash plant has two flowers: one male and one female." The sales clerk lifted one silver "flower" with her finger. "Bees must pollinate the flowers from one to the other. So the necklace is a symbol of fertility, procreation, and the continuation of life. All Indian women wore squash blossom necklaces."

"That's creepy," said Maggie. "You mean a woman wears this to become pregnant?"

"Well, yes. I guess you could say so. That was the hope anyway."

Alma had been studying the necklace from behind Maggie, and she now picked it up from the fake black neck and clasped it onto her own. Although Maggie thought the necklace would have looked prettier against Alma's black or white uniform than today's yellow one, she concluded that Alma looked regal. Her size matched the piece's majesty and showed Maggie what it was intended to look like. *If a gee-gaw could get you babies, this was it*, Maggie thought. Alma beamed at herself in the oval mirror mounted on the counter. She examined herself from the side, the front, and with her hands on her hips. The sales clerk held up her hands toward Alma's chest as if antsy to get the necklace off her, but Alma ignored her, preening.

"What about the horseshoe part?" Alma asked, pointing at the large centerpiece cradled between her bosoms.

"The crescent moon piece is called the Najah, and was patterned from Moorish decorations on bridles of the Spanish Conquistadors. They mounted the Najah between the horse's eyes to ward off the evil eye."

Alma half closed her chocolate pudding eyes. She tilted her chin slightly and studied the effect in the mirror.

"How much does it cost?" she asked the clerk.

"If you'll give it to me, I can read the price tag for you," the sales clerk said, her fingers again clawing toward the necklace. Maggie thought maybe the sales lady was jealous, because Alma for certain looked better in the necklace than she would, with her skinny shoulders and saggy chest.

Alma stalled and admired the necklace in the mirror another long time, so Maggie tried to distract the woman.

"Has anyone in town tried to sell you one of these recently?" Maggie asked.

"Pawned," corrected Alma.

"Not that I'm aware of," said the sales woman, "but you can ask the owner if you'd like. She's in the back. Perhaps I should call her." The woman glared at Alma and raised her hands again, as if she would either take the necklace off her or strangle her neck, which of course she wouldn't do because Alma was twice her size. Maggie suddenly wanted to grab one of the lady's long fingers and bend it backwards until it really hurt.

Alma fumbled with the necklace clasp and slowly removed it, ignored the woman's upraised hands and replaced it on the fraudulent black velvet neck. She smoothed it out so that all the silver trumpets lay straight, as if it were her own.

"No, I guess we don't need to talk to the owner now," said Maggie, storing her magnifying glass in her pocket. "But would you tell her that Maggie was here?"

"Maggie?" the woman asked.

"Maggie McGuire. Capital M small c capital G-u-i-r-e. And this is my housekeeper Hannah, who goes by Alma. We will be in town for a month, and if anyone tries to sell her a squash blossom necklace—with exceptional matrix—it is very important that she lets me know."

"Oh . . . I see," the sales clerk said, holding her hankie to her nose.

She stored the necklace securely away in the display case.

"But how could the owner let me know, if you don't ask us where we live?" said Maggie. "Or our telephone number?" Maggie picked up a receipt pad and pencil from the counter and wrote her name, and her grandmother's name.

"I'm sure the owner knows Jane Hamilton," said Maggie, handing the pad to her. "And in the event of any suspicious dealings regarding jewelry, I am the person to call."

Maggie turned to leave, but Alma hung back. She looked longingly at the necklace again, through the glass, reigning over its neighborhood of turquoise and silver bracelets, earrings and knuckle-to-knuckle-sized rings.

"That is a fine necklace. I want to get me one of those some day," Alma said, giving the gaping sales woman a wink and a nod.

7

Haunted Hotel by Horseback

AFTER A BREAKFAST of bacon and buckwheat pancakes that Alma had mastered, Maggie laid out on her bed the supplies for the horseback ride she had persuaded her new trial chums to take to the haunted hotel. She hoped to complete her horsewoman merit badge, having checked off several of the requirements at Girl Scout Camp earlier in the summer. If she could finish it and train two assistant detectives at the same time, it would be a banner day.

When Maggie chose the badges to pursue at camp, she noted with dismay that there were none labeled "detective" or "sleuthing" or "investigation," but perhaps after this summer she could create one herself and present the requirements to Mrs. Finney, her Girl Scout leader, to send to Girl Scout Headquarters.

Her pile included an extra bandana, a matchbox, a flashlight, her magnifying glass, a slicker, a thermos of water, her Brownie camera with extra flash cubes, her Girl Scout Handbook, and three Cherry Mash candy bars. She stuffed these into her Girl Scout knapsack.

Beyond the Girl Scout badge check-off, Maggie's goals were simple. She wanted to learn what made this hotel haunted, find out if it was still haunted, and see if her chums could even tell the difference.

The kids met at the dirt road behind their cabins that led to town. Maggie wore a long-sleeved western shirt, although the day was hot and dry, remembering how she was pestered by flies and mosquitoes when horseback riding at camp. She wore her red cowgirl hat, blue jeans, the red cowgirl boots that Grandpa had bought for her at Thunderbird's, and of course her fringed leather jacket, even though it was hot. She felt like she was outfitted swell until Jamie came into view dressed in a hard hat, a short-sleeved blouse, jodhpurs and tall riding boots. She carried a thin switch that she flicked a tad too close to Bebo's backside when she demonstrated how to use it, so that the two of them argued the entire way to the stable. Bebo tried to shoot Jamie's rear end with his bow and suction-cup-tipped arrows, reminding Maggie that she was mostly grateful to be an only child, and sad to be relinquishing that status in November.

They smelled the stable coming a block away. The horses were buddied up shoulder to shoulder in the coral chewing hay. The cool, dark barn held hay bales, horse tack hanging along the walls, and a small office with a half-door, which a wrangler came through.

He was bow-legged and dusty and wore a black cowboy hat with Buffalo-head nickels paraded along the hatband.

Jamie told the wrangler that they wanted horses for a half day. Bebo was a beginner and needed a gentle horse, but she was an experienced rider and would prefer an English saddle. Maggie stood right up next to her and said she was experienced too, and that a western saddle was fine with her. She knew the difference from her Girl Scout training and was thrilled that Jamie was looking like Miss Smarty Britches with little switches, which wouldn't play well on the rag-tag mix of quarter horses and Indian ponies out there pooping piles in the stable yard.

The wrangler walked among the lounging horses, matching them up for their ride. Sweat trickled down the sides of Maggie's face under her cowgirl hat, and she shielded her eyes from the dust that the wind kicked up off the bare ground.

First the wrangler outfitted Bebo with a sway-backed black mare called Geraldine, who lumbered up to him. The wrangler laced his fingers together for Bebo to step into and boosted him up onto the old mare's back, where Bebo clutched the reins and the saddle horn with both hands.

Next the wrangler led Maggie to a sleek brown quarter horse with a black main that he called Ricky D.

"What's the D for?" Maggie asked, as she stepped into the left stirrup and swung her right leg over his rump.

"Dynamite," replied the wrangler, spitting a brown stream into the dust.

Maggie's neck prickled with excitement.

Jamie deftly mounted a painted pony named Lil' Lulu, white with brown and black spots, equipped with the standard western saddle. She positioned both reins in her right hand, with her little finger separating the two, pulled the reins to turn Lil' Lulu's head to the right, and was on her way, in the lead, with her golden curls jostling on her shoulders under her riding hat. So stinkingly ND, thought Maggie, riding behind her.

"Bebo, you ride behind me so I can keep on eye on you," Jamie called, turning her head and pointing with her perky switch toward the behind of Lil' Lulu. Maggie's horse and Bebo's laid back their ears at each other until their pecking order was fixed, and the three ambled up Main Street waving at all the kids they passed.

At the end of town they left Main Street and entered the flats, a grassy meadow that was what remained of the Colorado River Valley not taken up by the reservoir. The horses knew the meadow and took off at a trot, then a lope, and then a flat out run. Ricky D did not disappoint Maggie, blasting past Geraldine, then past Lil' Lulu with Jamie posting up and down in rhythm with her trot. Maggie's legs hugged tightly to Ricky D's flanks, her hands gripped the saddle horn, and she flew with the wind, her hat held round her neck by it's string, her glasses like goggles in the wind, her leather fringe flying—abandonly and deliriously *free*.

As Ricky D approached the shore of the reservoir, an alarm registered in Maggie's brain. How would she stop him? Closer. Closer. She pulled on the reins, to no avail. Closer. Closer. Maggie pictured herself in a western movie. She would plunge into the lake, and Ricky D would swim, paddling his legs fiercely while keeping their heads above the water. Like dog paddllng. Horse paddling. No problem. Here they go. Closer. Closer. But ten feet from the shore Ricky D circled tightly and ran along the shore. Seems he didn't want to get his hooves wet.

As they turned back to re-cross the meadow, Maggie saw that Goldie Locks was not watching Bebo, unless she had eyes in the back of her hard hat. She flew on Lil' Lulu, leaning into the horse, her torso stretched out along her, as if Jamie had ridden Lil' Lulu all her life. It was a sight, Maggie had to admit. Bebo, meanwhile, bounced precariously atop Geraldine, his boots flopping up and down, with only his grasp on the saddle horn pinning him in place. Fortunately, Geraldine's fastest speed was an ungainly trot. "Yahoo! Yahoo!" Bebo yelled into the wind.

Back and forth they streaked between the road and the lakeshore, until the horses played out and cantered up to the lake to drink.

They let their horses feed in the tall grasses, then got back on the road to ride to the site of the decaying hotel on the lakeshore.

Maggie studied the site as they approached it, searching for anything exceptional. The view was, for sure: smack dab at the location where the postcard pictures were taken of Mt. Baldy, and where a long, sandy beach stretched into gradually deepening water.

"Looks like knocked down Lincoln Logs ," Bebo observed of the hotel. They had pulled their horses up alongside one another to dismount, and Bebo sat picking his nose until Jamie swatted his hand with her switch.

"I will tie up the horses," Maggie offered, this being one of the final Girl Scout requirements she needed to complete. She spaced out the horses and tied them each to a sturdy tree branch about the height of their mouths, using slip knots. She broke off any small branches that could poke them in the face, noted her process to Jamie, and asked Jamie if she would write down what Maggie had done and sign it off in her handbook.

"Oh, brother," Jamie said. "You write what you did and I'll just sign it."

Walking around the ruin, they saw that the second story of the log structure had caved in on the first. Only a massive stone chimney remained almost intact.

Nana had told Maggie that the hotel was haunted because four county commissioners were massacred there in the Wild West days. The shooting made the place so creepy that business had dwindled to nothing. Maggie figured that the hotel owners were so depressed over the whole thing, including the blood spots in their parlor and on the front porch, that they gave up and left it to decay. But, to Maggie's dismay, the rubble did not, at this point, sound, look or feel haunted. Nor were there still traces of blood.

"Pretty small for a hotel," observed Jamie.

"Yeah, but it would look bigger if it still had a top floor. You can't even tell how many bedrooms it had," said Maggie.

They sat on the beach eating Cherry Mashes, trying to decide if they should leave these Lincoln Logs and go back to riding their horses. Periodically Jamie flicked her switch at a mosquito or fly.

Jamie voted that they either go wading or go riding in the meadows some more. She got up, brushing the dirt from her jodhpurs and from her hands.

Her clear blue eyes met Maggie's, which Maggie hoped were steely gray today, because she sensed herself losing authority. "Let's take one thorough look around while we're here, okay?" Maggie said.

The porch boards had rotted away, so they stepped into the hotel over the door frame. Inside, two Christmas-tree-sized blue spruces grew up through a carpet of wood pulp and fungus on the rotted floor. The girls poked through the debris with sticks, looking for anything interesting or haunted-ish.

Meanwhile, Bebo had discovered a pile of animal scat in a corner and lobbed a piece at his sister, who chiseled away at one of the few surviving pieces of newspaper chinking in a wall.

"Ouch!" Jamie rubbed her ear. "Stop it, Bebo," she said, not bothering to see what he was throwing.

"I thought so," Jamie said to herself, "it's an old newspaper." She carefully unfolded a brittle fragment of darkened newsprint.

"Hey, look, I found something too!" Bebo exclaimed, bent over a pile of animal turds.

Maggie and Jamie took the brittle paper outside into better light, and Jamie gingerly spread it out on the ground. Maggie whipped out her magnifying glass from her blue jeans pocket and examined it closely. The scrap wasn't dated, nor did it include a headline, but it was from an old newspaper all right.

"Good work, Jamie," Maggie said, with a twinge of envy.

"Look . . . what . . . I . . . found!" Bebo stood before them with his grubby right hand palm up, fist clenched, his dirty fingernails resembling black-penciled semi-circles. He opened his feces-flecked hand to reveal a single silver bead, perfectly round and with a slim silver ridge around the center.

Maggie carefully pinched it between her thumb and index finger and rubbed it on her bandana, coaxing up a little shine. She pulled out her magnifying glass, which revealed what they already saw, with the addition of tiny nicks and scratches.

"Wow!" she said. "You know what this is, don't you?"

"Sure I know," said Bebo. "It's a silver bead from the Indian who murdered and scalped the county guys in this hotel."

Hard as it was to accept convincing evidence from someone with dirty fingernails and teeth missing, Maggie gave him her full attention.

Jamie sat on her haunches, wrote in the dirt with her switch, and ignored them.

"But the question is," Maggie said, taking charge, "did they find the murderers, or is this new evidence in an open case?"

"You're supposed to tell us, Nancy Drew," said Jamie.

Maggie ignored this comment and busied herself fetching her camera from her knapsack, and snapping close-up shots of the silver bead, displayed on her bandana, and also positioned near the pile of do-do where Bebo found it. Meanwhile, Bebo scraped through the scat pile with a stick to search for more beads, to no avail.

Maggie confiscated the bead from Bebo, arguing that she would need to give it to local authorities if the case was unsettled. Wrapping it in her bandana, she put it into her blue jeans pocket.

Maggie wanted to build on the sleuthing momentum of this find, but all Jamie and Bebo wanted to do now was to take off their boots, roll up their pants, and go wading before it was time to return their horses.

While they waded, Maggie sat on a boulder, staring at the sagging hotel that had coughed up a little treasure, imagining what the bead was from.

"Come on, Maggie. Give it up, can't you?" Jamie asked, swishing her hands around in the cool water. "You've got a silver bead—now can't you just play for awhile? Like a normal person?"

What if, Maggie wondered, from her rocky perch, what if this silver bead was a soiled remnant of a rare and beautiful squash blossom necklace worn by an opera singer who chanced to stay in this hotel on this picturesque lake on a fateful summer's day marred by murder and perhaps scalping?

Dear Diary,
Thursday, August 7, 1947

I am discovering that where the rubber meets the road in mysteries it goes forward, backward, forward, backward. Like today. In a real haunted hotel, which I don't see why they call it haunted except that its memories are definitely bad, we discovered an actual silver bead like from a squashed blossom necklace. This would cause a high degree of excitement in anybody with any sleuthing aptitude whatsoever, but all my chums wanted to do was knock it off and go wading.

Then, when we got home, Nana was mad as hops because the sheriff's deputy had been to the cabin snooping around as to why Alma and I would be asking so many questions about a squashed blossom necklace and give the shop lady a hard time. I have never heard Nana raise her voice higher than it would take to get across the room, but she raised it high and told me I was to drop the subject and let Mrs. Haggerty's missing necklace stay missing in peace. The lady hadn't asked me to solve her mystery, and it was none of my business.

I guess the real mystery to me is why the old lady doesn't seem to care. If one of those belonged to me, I'd flaunt it on my front whenever I went out to a big do, and would definitely worry if it were missing. How do you lose something that big? It's not like a watch or car keys. I think, with all due respect to the law, that Nana should have told the sheriff's deputy that it's a free country with freedom of speech and freedom of shopping, and he should mind his own business. I hope it doesn't work out that we need his services at the end of the case.

As for our great discovery, over dinner the Professor said that two white men had killed the county commissioners, not an Indian. And he suspects that the bead wasn't left by either an Indian or an opera singer, but was "deposited" by a treasure-eating wolf or coyote. Very funny. Now I agree with Nana, and hope he doesn't come over for dinner too often.

Alma suggested that tomorrow I take Nana trolling to show her a good time, and that I be on my best manners with her no matter how boring it gets. At least Grandpa will be happy with me if I do.

But there is no way that I can let a real mystery sleep. There is something funny about this old lady, Mrs. Haggerty. And I've got a real silver squashed blossom necklace bead right here in my bedside drawer. That has to mean something.

Sincerely,
Maggie

8

Trolling

BEFORE NANA AND Maggie arrived at the dock the next morning, every effort had been made to ensure the success of their venture. Grandpa had taught Maggie to drive the 12-foot aluminum outboard, the Hi-dee-ho. He had filled the motor with gas at the marina and had gathered all the fishing gear they could possibly need, storing it inside the small open boat. Alma came to see them off and handed Maggie her life vest and a slicker, and passed to Nana a picnic basket stocked with meatloaf sandwiches, potato chips, oatmeal cookies, and a thermos of sweetened iced tea.

Nana wore a wide-brimmed straw sun hat, denim dungarees, a short-sleeved blouse, clean white sneakers, and carried her knitting bag over her shoulder, which made Maggie think that her company, and fishing, might not be quite enough for Nana. Granted, any one activity in a little aluminum boat might feel cramped after a few minutes. Maggie had on a sun suit and a sweatshirt to start out, with her hair freshly brushed into a tidy ponytail.

"You're in for some fine fishing today," Alma said. "Bet I'll have more trout to cook from you tonight than I'll have from Mr. Hamilton."

"He doesn't think so," said Maggie. "Grandpa doesn't think there's any skill to lake fishing. I heard him tell the Professor that he thought Nana would be out here trailing her hook behind the boat, working crossword puzzles or filing her fingernails."

"Why, Maggie, he wouldn't say that," Nana objected.

"He sure did." Maggie didn't like it when her grandmother contradicted her, as if Maggie was lying or didn't know what she was hearing.

"Well, we'll just show him then," countered Nana, stowing her knitting bag clear into the bow of the boat.

"What would make him eat his words?" Maggie asked.

"Maggie, you shouldn't talk like—" Nana began.

"How's about you catch the bigger trout today? Bring me one that curls his tail over the edge of my big skillet!" Alma trilled her fingers in a high arch. She had on her aqua uniform, since it was Friday.

"All right, we will," said Nana. "Let's get on with it."

Maggie gunned the motor. Nana pitched backwards, one hand securing the top of her sun hat and the other grabbing a gunwale as they lurched from the dock into a smooth, blue lake on a cloudless August morning.

"Where do you want to go, Nana?"

"Well," Nana surveyed the lake, "we could crowd around the channel with those other fishing boats, in case they know something we should know, or we can go someplace by ourselves. What do you think?"

"Maybe we try the channel first and get some free lessons," said Maggie. "Then we definitely go off by ourselves."

Maggie steered toward the channel at three-quarters speed. As they neared it, she threaded the outboard around the other boats, avoiding the fishing lines, looking for a good position, until a fat man with suspenders and a slouchy hat growled at her. "Hey, girl! Cut your motor!"

"Okay, okay!" Maggie yelled back. All heads in boats turned in their direction, and some fishermen moved their boats to give them wider berth.

"Maggie, that was rude," Nana whispered.

"Well, Nana, I'm trying!"

"Okay, Maggie, let's just let the engine idle and start fishing."

Grandpa had set the lines with lures. They each flung theirs over a different side of the boat, then sat and watched the red and white bobbers dimple the surface of the water. They watched a fisherman reel in a fish and reach into the water with his net to scoop up the shiny flapping creature. And they sat and watched the other fishermen sitting and watching.

"Kinda wish I'd brought my book," said Maggie. Nana did not reply, and did not reach for her knitting bag. She sat up tall.

A thrill erupted when they thought Maggie had a bite, only to discover her lure was caught in seaweed on the bottom. To precipitate some needed action they launched out, trailing their lines behind them as they cruised up the lakeshore.

Maggie steered the Hi-dee-ho in a margin far enough from shore to keep their lines unencumbered, but close enough that they could get a good look at the shoreline cabins and boathouses. Nana kept motioning for her to keep closer to shore; Maggie kept giving the boat its head, which seemed to want to move out lake.

"Nana, which one is Mrs. Haggerty's cabin?" Maggie asked.

"Why? I thought we were finished with the drama of the squash blossom necklace."

"I was just wondering, since she is one of the few people I have met on this lake," said Maggie. "And where is Mrs. Wyatt's house?"

"They're still a ways off," Nana said vaguely.

Nana's bobber disappeared below the surface. She stared at the line, immobilized, but it came again—a definite tug.

"Nana, bring it in!" yelled Maggie.

"Shhhhhhhh. You'll scare him off!"

"But you'll let him off!" whispered Maggie. "Pull on it!"

As Nana reeled in the line, Maggie grabbed the net and leaned over the side of the boat. She hauled the fish into the boat and they stared at it as it struggled to get free of the net.

"It's too little," breathed Nana.

"I know. What do we do?"

"We have to let it go."

"How?"

"Take the hook out of its mouth."

"You do it," said Maggie.

"No, you."

The fish eyeball stared at them, pleading.

Maggie practiced touching the slippery fish-child, then grasped it loosely so that it wriggled out of her hand, then grasped it with determination and gingerly worked the hook out as the fish flipped his head back and forth.

"Oh!" cried Maggie, as the hook came free and in reflex she tossed the saved creature, but missed the side so it fell back into the bottom of the boat.

Nana held her feet high and tried to retrieve the fish with the net while Maggie groped with her hands. "Beep, beep! If you would move your bottom, Nana, I could get to him," Maggie nudged her over so she could sit next to Nana and get a grip on the fish. Finally the creature lay panting on its side and Maggie grasped him and completed the rescue.

Without Maggie's attention the boat had circled itself back toward home so she had to get it on course again. They slumped on their seats panting and sweating.

Nana breathed deeply. "Do you think we can do this?"

"Well, we just did, didn't we," Maggie said, and they laughed together. Nana's dimples were showing!

"As long as you think it's fun, Nana, we'll keep going."

"We'll give it a good try and see."

They decided to fish with one line and so stored Maggie's. Taking a fresh lure from the tackle box, Maggie tied it onto Nana's line with a snappy square knot from her Girl Scout repertoire.

The next trout to tug on their line was dinner-worthy. Nana reeled him in, Maggie swooped it into the boat in the net, then Maggie held the slippery creature while Nana removed the hook from its mouth. Splash! It went into the pail of water in the bow of the boat.

By late morning they peered down at three respectable captives, and admired their glistening scales and the fleck of rainbow along their bellies as they swam in detention in their pail. Maggie felt attached to the fish. They were pets that she wouldn't have to feed: and in fact, vice versa.

Then the novelty wore off. Fish quit biting, and they grew bored. Maggie made a game of driving the boat up close to submerged boulders or shallow ledges and veering away at the very last minute. Nana complained that Maggie didn't need to be so dramatic, at which Maggie bristled and said if Nana would rather drive the boat, she could. This was smarty, and it drew down Nana's turtle eye. Maggie felt trapped now in the little boat on a hot day. By this time she'd removed her sweatshirt and they'd poured themselves some iced tea.

"Shall we call it a day?" Maggie asked.

"We can't go back before lunchtime," Nana said. So they declared it was lunchtime and broke out the chips and sandwiches.

As they ate, Nana gave Maggie tidbits about the summer people who lived in the cabins they passed. Many of them were from Texas or Oklahoma or Kansas, like they were.

"When did you get your cabin?" Maggie asked as she chewed.

"When your mother was fourteen, and Max was just a toddler," said Nana. "We'd been vacationing here, renting a small cabin, and your grandfather had discovered fly-fishing. We were watching for a place."

"How much did it cost?" asked Maggie.

"That is not something for children to know," Nana replied stiffly. Turtle eye number two.

"I mean, did you get a good deal?"

"Yes, yes we did," Nana nodded.

"I often wished my teen summers had been as romantic as your mother's were here," Nana said, as she finished her sandwich and dabbed her mouth with a napkin.

"They were? Romantic?"

Nana laughed softly. "Oh, yes. Just up the shore from here lived a young man Adele danced with at the Pine Cone Inn. After the band quit for the night, they'd go on moonlight boat rides. She was only sixteen, and I probably shouldn't have let her, but. . . ." Nana sighed.

"I used to sit on the porch in the cabin in the dark, watching until the boat's headlight appeared and pulled up to our dock. Once I saw Adele's flashlight beam bouncing up the steps to the house, I stole upstairs to bed." Nana paused. "Unless, that is, it was so late that I needed to talk to her." She winked at Maggie.

Maggie was so surprised that she studied Nana's face but decided yes, it was certainly a wink.

When they passed the cabin of Adele's long-ago boyfriend, Nana pointed out lights twinkling far into the house, and Maggie cut the motor so they could drift past it. "Does Daddy know about the summer boyfriend?" Maggie asked.

"I suppose so," said Nana.

"What happened?" Maggie asked.

"To the boyfriend?" asked Nana.

"No, I mean to Mother. I can't picture her kissing in a boat. Or climbing the steps in the dark with a flashlight. I can picture her fixing a pot roast for dinner and sweeping the back steps. And napping on the davenport."

As Nana considered this, her eyebrows pinched together. "Well, I guess your daddy happened. And you happened. And then your mother's miscarriages happened. And then your daddy was away in the war, so your mother lost her time for dancing."

"You all right, Maggie?" Nana asked when she grew quiet.

"I was thinking about my parents dancing. Once I went to a dance with them, and they looked like in the movies. Not the stars in the movies, but regular people dancing like the stars danced in the movies.

"I danced with Daddy, but he did a funny bounce from the knees and I was always going up while he was coming down. But I'll be a good dancer someday," Maggie said, and imagined running up the steps with a flashlight after a moonlight boat ride.

The boat drifted for a while. By now the sunshine had drawn out boaters of all ilk, who passed them in one direction or the other: canoes, outboards, sleek wooden Chris Crafts, and even the Showboat, the marina's tourist launch. As it passed, the wake of the Showboat rolled beneath the Hi-dee-ho, and they held to the gunwales as the boat swung crazily back and forth. Maggie could hear the patter of the tourist guide and swept her gaze to the shore when she heard—

"—longtime summer home of Mrs. and Mrs. Walter Haggerty of Norman, Oklahoma. . . ."

Maggie gunned the motor. She swept around in a wide circle, took the Showboat's wake head-on, and aimed for the Haggerty's dock.

"Maggie, we're not stopping here," Nana said anxiously. "I thought you just wanted to see where it was."

"You weren't going to tell me, were you Nana? I don't need to go to the door. I just want to stop long enough to make some observations."

"But Maggie!" Nana yelled, over the boat motor. "You don't just park at someone's dock and gawk."

"Nana, I never gawk," Maggie said, coming at the dock too fast, so that the bow of the boat banged it, throwing them backwards. Maggie held onto the metal ring on the dock and looked the place over. Nana turned around to face out lake, obviously hoping not to be recognized from the house.

After several moments of sitting rigid, looking away, Nana turned her head to whisper. "What do you see? Are you quite finished?"

"The door from the porch to the house is wide open, so Mrs.

Haggerty is at home. And there's a maid's cabin out back. . . .I should interview Coralee too."

"Interview?" Nana hissed. "Mrs. Haggerty is an elderly lady, Maggie, and we need to respect her privacy. I really don't think this is appropriate, and I wish you would respect my wishes and let it be."

"Don't you want her to find her necklace?"

"Well of course, but she probably just misplaced it, and it will turn up. Old people do that, Maggie."

"But maybe by talking about it with her we can help her remember where she put it."

Maggie let go of the dock and pulled the chord to start the engine. As they pulled away, Maggie looked back and noticed that a figure watched them from an upstairs bedroom window.

"Maggie, if you continue this foolishness, I am going to have to tell your mother," Nana said. As if that would make a difference.

Maggie opened the motor full throttle, heading the Hi-dee-ho for home.

Alma came to the dock when she heard the boat return.

"Mmm Mmm Mmm! They're fat and sassy ones," Alma said, with her eyes crinkled and her teeth smiling, until she detected the gloom draped over the craft. She quietly relieved them of their trout and jiggled her bulk up the stone steps to the cabin, nodding to herself.

At dinner, Grandpa patted Nana's hand and said they'd made a splendid catch for their first time out. He had to admit that they were tastier than his. But when the Professor pointed out that lake trout were always fatter than stream trout, because they got their food lazily and didn't have to work as hard, Nana threw up her hands and got pouty.

"Hey," Maggie said. "You can't blame us for that. Besides, Nana did not take out her knitting or her crossword puzzles."

"Well of course I didn't," Nana protested.

Maggie was joking, but she let it go, knowing that Nana was touchy. The house was in a hub-bub because Uncle Max was on his way.

Max Hits the Lake

Maggie watched over Alma's shoulder as she deciphered her list for the day. which Nana had written on a bridge tally sheet. A cup of coffee steamed at Alma's elbow. Snugged up under the lapels of Alma's white uniform was a bolo tie from Thunderbird's with a turquoise mounted in the slide. Alma said it was the closest she could come to a squash blossom necklace for now.

The list was complicated and full: Grandpa's food for a fishing pack trip leaving at 9:00 a.m., serving bridge club at 10:00 a.m., cleaning the bathrooms in the afternoon, and preparing the day's three meals, including lamb chops and wilted lettuce salad for dinner—Nana's favorites, since Grandpa would be gone.

"Did you write these names?" Maggie asked. Above each column a family name had been written in pencil: Mr. Hamilton, Mrs. Hamilton, Miss Maggie, and Mr. Max.

"Yes, I did."

"What do the numbers underneath them mean?"

Alma pursed her generous pink lips. She wore her big silver hoop earrings and tight curls escaped her bandana along her forehead.

"Well, since the sheet was labeled 'Individual Scores,' I thought

I would take a few minutes before this busy day began to figure a Vacation Score for each person so far," Alma explained.

"Oh?" Maggie asked. "Why is my score a three?"

"Well, you and your grandmother are sittin' so-so in your gettin' along, and you're on a solving-a-mystery track toward a 5 unless you get in the way of it."

"Grandpa's already a five?"

"He's gone fishing eeeeevry day."

"Nana is only a 2+. What does the plus mean?"

"Your grandmother will be movin' up shortly, if she just lets herself know some fun when she sees it."

"Why is Uncle Max even on here? He just arrived last night."

"We've got to hold a place for Mr. Max, and he'll fill it directly. So I gave him a 1 to start him off."

"Why is Baxter written off in the margin with a question mark?"

"Well, you see I haven't heard from Baxter," Alma replied, then paused. "I would very much like to know how's I can replace that question mark with a positive score." Maggie put her arm around Alma's neck and hugged her tight, and Alma hung onto the hug.

Later, when Maggie came downstairs dressed for the morning— she changed her clothes three or four times a day because the weather changed or her swimsuit was wet—Nana was waving good-bye to the fishermen and Alma had set the bridge table for four in the living room. Maggie offered to help Alma whip up a batch of Arkansas Hot Pepper Pecans while Nana picked up magazines and books and settled things as she liked them to look.

When the ladies arrived, Maggie slipped past her grandmother to read on the porch, but Nana caught her wrist.

"Maggie, won't you greet our guests?"

"Hello," she smiled quickly.

"Hello, Maggie," said Tilly Wyatt. "I hear you and your grand-mother are quite a fishing team."

"And our children had such fun on their horseback ride," said pretty Mrs. Gerrard.

"We found something at the haunted hotel," Maggie said. "I'll show you."

Maggie ran upstairs to fetch the silver bead. She opened its bandana at the bridge table, and they all peered over their reading glasses at the treasure.

"Is this like the beads on your squashed blossom necklace?" Maggie asked Mrs. Haggerty, because the moment seemed happy.

"Squash blossom? Why, I believe it is."

"The necklaces break rather easily, you know," said Mrs. Gerrard. "The Indians used string from feed sacks. Mine broke once. Luckily I found all the beads and took it to Miller's Indian Village in Estes Park for repair."

This was interesting to Maggie. Mrs. Haggerty coughed a hacky few coughs and cleared her throat. She clawed through her pocketbook for a tissue and held it to her mouth.

"Are you all right, Louise?" Nana asked.

Mrs. Haggerty nodded, but seemed to withdraw into her C curve.

"Mrs. Haggerty, you haven't found your necklace yet, have you?" Maggie asked.

"No, I haven't," Mrs. Haggerty snapped. She stared at her playing cards and lifted one with a boney finger to discard.

"Did you maybe take it in for repair?" asked Maggie.

"No, I did not," she said with finality.

"Well, I hear that playing bridge is good for old people's brains, so if you have misplaced it and you think of it after bridge, would you please let me know?" Maggie smiled, but Nana turned her fan of cards face down on the table and turned a turtle-eye to Maggie.

"Maggie, please apologize to Mrs. Haggerty, and then why don't you go to the kitchen and see if Alma has something for you to do," said Nana, fake-calmly.

"But, I didn't mean—" Maggie began.

Mrs. Haggerty shifted her eyes from her cards for a quick glance at Maggie.

"I'm sorry, Mrs. Haggerty. I only meant it's good that you play bridge," said Maggie, and headed for the kitchen just as Max came down the stairs. He sauntered past the bridge table toward the kitchen, scratching the frolicking cowlick in the back of his red hair. He was dressed in a t-shirt, pajama bottoms and an open flannel bathrobe.

"Morning, ladies," he wiggled the fingers with which he had scratched his head. "Late night trip, you know. Sorry to disturb you." He kept walking and pushed through the swinging door into the kitchen.

Holding the skillet handle with a folded kitchen towel, Alma stood at the stove tossing the Arkansas Hot Pepper Pecans in a cast-iron skillet. She replaced the skillet onto the metal burner, wiped her hands on her apron and greeted him with a welcome-to-the-cabin hug.

"I'm famished, Alma," he said. "How about a hearty mountain breakfast? Bacon, fried eggs, pancakes."

"Mr. Max, I've got about all I can handle here without fixing another breakfast at half past ten in the morning."

"Well, what am I supposed to eat? My last food was in Colby, Kansas."

"Mr. Max, I don't care how many mouths I have to feed at any meal; the more the merrier, that's what I say. I would be happy to fix you a big mess of breakfast tomorrow morning. But when a meal is past, it's past, and this train is moving on to the next stop, and that would be Arkansas Hot Pepper Pecans for the bridge ladies, followed by lunch."

Max stood looking out the window over the sink at the cabin next-door, ignoring Alma while she fussed at him. He scratched his head. He scratched his rear. Then he turned to look at her.

"I'll bet that maid next door will fix me some breakfast," Max said, yawning. He walked out the back porch door and over to the next cabin, where Francine was sweeping the back steps.

"Mr. Max, do not ask Francine to do such a thing!" Alma said, following close behind him.

"Hi dee ho, Francine isn't it?" Max asked as he walked up the stairs.

"Why, yes, sir," she said.

"I was wondering, I hate to disrupt your sweeping, but would you have some breakfast vitals you could whip up for a starving man who drove half the night over Berthoud Pass in the rain?"

Francine held onto the broom and looked quizzically at Alma, who was scowling. "Well, I'd imagine so . . ."

"Now aren't you folks from Texas," Max chattered as he followed Francine into the house, "—two young ladies here, I recall . . . cousins?"

And of course while this nonsense was going on next door, Alma's Arkansas Hot Pepper Pecans got too hot and dark on the stove. She came back into the kitchen in a flutter, dumped this batch in the trashcan on the back porch, opened the window so the stink would travel outside instead of to the bridge table, and started over.

"Why is it when Mr. Max arrives the Cracker Jacks fly out of the box?" Alma muttered.

Then she seemed to see Maggie for the first time. "What is it, Miss Maggie? Did your grandmother send you in here?"

"She thought you might have something for me to do. Which is silly. When have I ever had trouble finding something to do?"

"Well, I suspect something quiet would be the thing just now, with your mystery book or the jigsaw puzzle." Alma raised her eyebrows and cocked her head toward the kitchen door, from which Maggie was only too glad to escape.

Maggie settled at the jigsaw puzzle on the card table on the porch, a circular puzzle of different dastardly pirates, their ships and treasures. She hoped for invisibility. From her vantage point she could see what was happening out on the lake, and hear what was talked about at the bridge table. When she grew bored of the puzzle, Maggie

75

picked up the first book she found handy, which was *A Tree Grows in Brooklyn* with Nana's pressed wildflower bookmark half-way through it.

At first there was little talk from the table. Maybe they knew where Maggie was sitting and hadn't yet forgotten her.

Then Max came in the screened porch door in a rush.

"Were the girls home, Uncle Max?" Maggie teased, looking up from her book.

"Yep. Two dolls, with accents thicker 'n' sweeter than pancake syrup," Uncle Max pulled on Maggie's pigtail in passing.

Soon Uncle Max passed her again, dressed in a swimsuit and sneakers with a towel around his neck. His hair was combed and Brylcreemed. He took the stone steps to the lake two at a time, his Kodak swinging from his shoulder. On the dock, Max parked himself in the swing and surveyed the water stretching in front of him, still so morning-smooth that each individual pine tree on the mountain up the opposite shore was reflected in it. He sat with his legs stretched out in front of him and his arms resting on the back of the swing. On the screened porch, Maggie watched, pretended to read, and listened.

"Where'd you get this recipe, Alma? These are the best peppered pecans."

"Why, thank you, ma'am. They're a little something my mama taught me to make."

"Jane, how is Adele?"

"Doing fine, according to her last letter. Still on bed rest. You know it was these middle months when she had her miscarriages. Jack's selling life insurance. He says there's great potential, but we haven't seen it yet. Poor Adele."

On the dock Max stood to snap some shots just as Maggie saw the two Texas teenagers next door walk down to their dock. The brunette wore a culotte sun suit, a wide-brimmed straw sun hat tied under her chin with a scarf, and black sunglasses. The other, a blond, had on a yellow swimsuit. As she stood on her dock and waved at Max, her buxom body parts bounced with excitement.

Max waved back and disappeared into the boathouse.

"John is coming this weekend, but as you can imagine all these steps are difficult with his prosthesis," said Norma Gerrard. *John must be Jamie and Bebo's dad*, Maggie thought. *What part did he not have? A leg? A foot? Why hadn't they told her?*

A metallic whine told Maggie that Max was taking out Grandpa's Chris Craft, named after her mother, who'd had the dancing boyfriend.

The Adele roared to life, belching spray behind her. Maggie watched the boat emerge from the boathouse into the summery world with Max driving and a pair of water skis propped against the backseat.

"Must be Max," Nana said to the bridge ladies. "Frank wanted to take him out and show him a few things about the boat before he took it out alone. Oh, well!"

"If he'd been in the service, you wouldn't say such a thing, Jane," Tilly said. "My Jeffrey, why, doesn't occur to us there's anything he can't do."

As Maggie watched, the girl in the yellow swimsuit stuffed her hair into a yellow rubber swim cap with a large daisy on the side. She tugged the elastic of her yellow swimsuit down over her rear-end, and the suit squeezed out pillows of flesh on her thighs.

Then the yellow swimsuit girl sat down on the end of the dock, lifting her rump from side to side till she was out on the very edge. Meanwhile, Max put the Adele in neutral out about eight feet from the dock and moved to the back of the boat to toss the water skis into the water, floating them toward the yellow swimsuit girl. The other girl stooped down and caught the tip of one of them, but the other veered off and floated beyond her grasp.

"Ut oh," said Maggie, running to the porch door and down the steps to the lake, where her services were needed, and so she didn't hear Nana say . . .

"Louise, I've been thinking. I do apologize for Maggie's behavior. I know it's been distressing to you, but I'm wondering if you could encourage the girl a bit. As a favor. She needs to have something to do. . . ."

10

Shifting the Column

MAGGIE WASN'T MUCH for sunbathing; she preferred to wade and catch minnows in a pail. She stood with her pail in calf-deep water, with her knobby knees, her protruding tummy and the two small bulges in her upper swimsuit. When she stood up straight and sucked in, she could see her knees; when she didn't, she couldn't.

Jamie, lying on her yellow and green-striped beach towel, had a definite waist and definite b-words. Susan, the culotte girl, showed off her curves today, sunning in a navy blue two-piece swimsuit with a white bow at one shoulder. Teensy's parts again were squeezed into the yellow swimsuit, and mushroomed out the edges.

Maggie hoped to someday have a waist, like Scarlet O'Hara in *Gone with the Wind*, which she had read the juicy parts of to her friends at naptime in her tent at Girl Scout Camp. The bosom thing she wasn't so excited about, but it seemed to be a package deal.

Presently Francine brought down some bottles of Orange Crush. Then she settled in the gazebo with Alma, the two of them stretching their legs out into the sunshine, talking and laughing. Maggie spread her towel next to Jamie's and sat down cross-legged to drink her pop.

"Jamie," Maggie said.

"Hmmm?"

"What happened that your dad has a protagonist?"

Jamie rolled over on her side to face Maggie and raised her sunglasses to frown at her.

"Come on, Maggie, it's a prosthesis. Or just call it a fake leg."

Dang, thought Maggie. Dumb again.

"Oh. Yes. Well, how . . . ?" Maggie asked.

"He got his left leg blown off in the war. So it's just a stump, with a flap of skin capped over it. Above his knee." Jamie drew her finger across her thigh to show where she meant.

"Does he talk much about what happened?" Maggie asked.

"Never," said Jamie. "Just says so many guys got so much worse that he's grateful to be alive. Mother says that's why he works so hard at the hospital." Jamie put her sunglasses back on and laid on her back. "But I wish he could be here more."

The wind was rising, so that the flags snapped briskly on the flagpoles. Maggie watched a motorboat skim past them, and thought how thankful she was to be alive, on a lake, with two strong legs and a mystery to solve. The sun seared her back and shoulders and prickled her scalp where her hair was parted for pigtails. On the shore Alma and Francine chortled in the gazebo.

Grandpa returned from his pack trip about four o'clock, and waddled bow-legged from the car to the cabin. Nana and Alma had conferred in the kitchen about which neighbors would want the extra trout. But Grandpa's creel hung slim, and he sagged too.

He'd caught four trout, in fact—just enough for dinner with Nana's morning contribution of two from the lake. Maggie was acquiring a taste for trout, especially since Alma knew to cut off the head for her and just put the body on her plate. Grandpa acted tired and cranky during dinner, and the Professor didn't join them.

"Blast it, I wish I hadn't waited to write the Willow until tonight," he muttered, poking his forkful of trout into a pillow of mashed potatoes. "But I thought I'd get some good material."

"I keep telling you I'll write it for you," Nana said. "And, boy do I ever have material."

"Just let it be, Janie," Grandpa said. "I'm not in the mood to talk about it."

After Maggie helped Alma with the dishes, which meant singing and general kitchen carrying-on, they came to the living room where Grandpa stood in front of the fireplace, with a stack of newsprint on the mantel and a pencil in his hand. Nana sat on the davenport knitting, and Maggie and Alma settled themselves at the card table for double solitaire. Grandpa's bald head and his nose and cheeks were the color of a rare steak. So much for always wearing his hat.

"What are you doing, Grandpa?" Maggie asked.

"I am cursing the pain in my buttocks and thighs and the small of my back and the awkward, non-shock-absorbing, stiff-jointed, cruel nag that got me this way," he growled, but his eyes twinkled at her. Grandpa loved to play with words, and she could tell he was warming up.

Perhaps to milk their sorrow, Grandpa read aloud as he wrote his column:

Yesterday I took my first horseback ride. Not the first this season, but the first in a lifetime. And it wasn't a little jaunt up a marked trail. It was a 12-mile hunt for a lake in a crater just below timberline. Seven hours in the saddle over two days!

At a distance I've always admired horses; they give the impression of being beautiful, graceful and intelligent beasts. Worthy of my daughter's unchallenged worship until boyfriends muscled into her heart.

"I love horses too, Grandpa," Maggie interjected.

Grandpa nodded without looking at Maggie. "Oh, you do," he said absently. Then he continued writing.

Now I know better. A horse is a beast of burden—and he should be nothing else. He should spend the rest of his declining days in the harness; not the saddle and bridle—the harness, I insist, the harness!

A horse wasn't created to ride—he was brought into this world to pull plows and wagons and cultivators.

"Amen!" called Alma.

"What do you know?" laughed Maggie.

"Why, I grew up around horses, Baby Girl."

Life is too short to be spent in driving 1,000 miles in a motorcar in order to pay for the privilege of suffering the agonies of riding a horse!

The Professor's horse, half way up the trail, after maneuvering a deep bog, bent his knees and lay flat in the wooded path. I didn't blame him. I was tempted to lie down beside him.

"Frank . . . Frank!" Nana protested. Maggie and Alma looked up from their cards. Grandpa paused, his pencil dripping with horse vengeance.

"Frank," Nana said gently. "Will you please let me write your column for you? I've offered many times, and you told me maybe on vacation."

Grandpa rubbed his face all over. He sighed.

"All right, all right. But this one I'll dictate to you since I'm nearly finished."

"Let's hope so," Nana said, poking her knitting needles into the growing yellow baby blanket. She moved to the typewriter on the desk in the corner, straightened his paper piles in a flurry, then settled her rump—wiggling it as Alma and Maggie laughed—into his desk chair.

"Proceed," Nana said. She stuck a pencil behind her right ear, and poised her hands above the typewriter keys.

"Show off!" said Grandpa, who could only type with his index fingers.

It took Grandpa a few minutes to rev his brain again, so Nana relaxed her fingers, bent them like she was playing the piano, straightened them to examine her nail polish, then bent them again. "Let's get off the horse, Frank. I think we're finished with that." He ignored her and continued.

Now for the trip to Bowen Lake. This hidden mountain pool is at the bottom of a 1,000-foot crater, above timber line and surrounded by snow banks, about twenty miles from Grand Lake.

"Twelve," Nana corrected.
"Twelve what?"
"Twelve miles from Grand Lake."
"Well, it sure felt like twenty miles."

The beauty of its setting surpasses anything I have yet seen in my years of limited variations. Only the thrill of these almost supernatural creations of nature prevented me from lying down, on the first leg of our journey, and sending word to the rangers to come and get me.

Nana rolled her eyes.
"Well, it's lovely," she said, "except for the 'limited variations.' Kansans will find that a slam, won't they, Frank?"
"But I'm a Kansan, and I've never in my life seen so many variations as here, that is certainly true," Alma interjected.
"If anything, it's a generous way to say we went from wheat fields to purple mountain majesties, I should think. Can we do this without your comments, do you s'pose? At least until the end? Which my body is about to?" Grandpa left the fireplace and eased himself into the armchair. Then he continued.

Bowen Lake is alive with hungry trout. And what beauties! All of 'em fourteen inches and longer.

We scarcely noticed the gusts of cold wind off the glaciers at our first glimpse of fish darting around in the icy water. At one time I saw three big trout nosing my flies.

But two hours of casting in a lake full of hungry trout convinced me I wasn't patterned to be a fisherman. Here they were—out of food and penned up in a mountain crater—and I caught only four!

"The Professor was high man for the day with eleven," Nana read as she added this in. Grandpa frowned.

We ate expensive fish at our cabin tonight. I figure they cost us $3.75 each, what with the expense of the horses. And, of course, now there's the torment. There may yet be doctors' bills to add, I am figuring, as I stand writing this on the fireplace mantel.

Tomorrow will be the first day I haven't been out with creel and landing net hanging over my shoulder and flapping boots sloshing in the stream. And I wouldn't go if I knew, down in a pool a grandpap was waiting for me—a grandpap weighing four pounds, with whiskers of a dozen leaders sticking from his jaws.

"So what's your take-away here?" Nana asked. She turned to look at Grandpa, crossing her arms.

"Beg pardon?"

"So your backside hurts because you rode your first horse. And the fish eluded you. Big deal." Nana threw up her hands. "I will defer to your judgment, of course, Frank. This is your column and you're a master at it. But I think we should consider the bigger story."

"And what might that be, my dear?" Grandpa asked, tamping down tobacco into his pipe.

"Well, when I went trolling today, as I caught four lazy lake fish, what do you think I saw floating past me into the lake out of the channel to Shadow Mountain Reservoir?"

"A canoe paddle?" Grandpa guessed wearily.

"No."

"The top to a bikini," Maggie guessed.

"Nope."

"A tree trunk with a beaver sitting on top," Alma volunteered.

"A head of lettuce!" Nana exclaimed.

"A head of lettuce?" Grandpa repeated.

"Did you know, Frank, that the sewage from the town of Grand Lake used to empty into the Colorado River from the flats just past the channel? And so, now that the water is being pumped through the channel into Grand Lake and on to Estes, the muck is flowing right into the lake with it!"

"And how did you learn this?" Grandpa asked.

"At the drug store, when I told the man behind me in line about the head of lettuce. I think we should expose this in the Willow, and I intend to do more research in town," Nana said. "I knew it would make exceptional column material."

"Yes, but will the good folks of Topeka be interested?" Grandpa asked.

"More than are interested in the condition of your buttocks, I should say! I think people should be concerned. It's a starting place."

"Then why don't *you* participate on the town committee the Professor is badgering me about?"

"How about I'll write the Willows and you join the committee? You're who they want, Frank. Surely it won't take that much of your time."

Grandpa sat puffing on his pipe. He let the smoke coil out of the sides of his mouth, climb up his crimson face and dissipate into the air.

Crossword Puzzle

RAIN, RAIN, RAIN on Wednesday. Alma could barely see the dark bulk of the mountains across the lake, looming behind a gray curtain of drizzle. She built a fire in the fireplace first thing after putting coffee on to perk.

Grandpa and the Professor had gone fishing, although Nana predicted they'd end up sitting on the boardwalk in front of Thunderbird's. Max was still sleeping. His pattern was cards or water skiing with the girls next door in the afternoons, and out to the Pine Cone Inn at night.

Still in her white bathrobe and with her hair in pin curls, Nana sat at the desk punching the keys of Grandpa's typewriter: click, click, click. As Alma poked the fire, Nana pulled her day's schedule from the typewriter, handed it to Alma, and scrolled in a new sheet of paper.

Alma took a seat to rest her bunions and read her marching orders. "What are you doing this early, Miz Hamilton?" she asked.

"I've got to get this column in shape before the morning mail goes out," Nana replied, typing with gusto.

"I thought you finished it last night."

Nana paused and looked at Alma over her reading glasses. "I'm the columnist now, and I will not send out all that horse drivel."

"So what are you writing, Nana?" Maggie asked, sitting cross-legged in front of the fire.

"Just a minute. I'm almost done, and then I'll read it to you."

Nana pulled the newsprint from the typewriter with a zip and held it up to read aloud.

While your regular editor and columnist is fly-fishing on the streams, storing up the beauty of the Rockies and snagging trout for our dinner table, I am honored to write this column for him. My purpose is to give you a respite from your daily occupations, writing from the magnificent cool heights of this mountain clime.

At a time when Americans are eager to vacation again, how pleasant it was to return to Grand Lake, after a hiatus during the war years. We found the village bustling and prosperous, welcoming vacationers from near and far.

The Colorado-Big Thompson Project has added a large reservoir for fishing and boating to this region, with another under construction. The surfaced highways and influx of labor for this ambitious water diversion project have made the beauty of this area accessible to both summer and winter travelers.

August in Grand Lake is proving the wettest recalled by old timers, but it cannot dampen your editor's fishing forays with Edgar Duvall, a retired pharmacist and local expert on angling.

Meanwhile, we are cozy at home with the frequent companionship at the bridge table of Mrs. Walter Haggerty of Oklahoma City; Mrs. Erwin Wyatt of Austin, Texas; and Mrs. John Gerrard of Denver.

The sailboat races have begun, and frequent squalls on the lake can whip them quickly from drifters to big blows. Our son Maxwell, photographer on the paper, will be a valiant competitor on the E-scow, The Dame.

"What do you think?" Nana asked, removing her glasses and turning to face them. She examined the nail on her right index finger, which had taken a beating on the typewriter keys.

"Couldn't you include one of Grandpa's funny parts, like wanting to lie down in the path like the horse?" Maggie asked.

"Definitely not. It's beneath your grandfather as editor of the paper." Nana sat up taller, as if doing it for him.

"But where's the lettuce, Nana? I thought that was your big deal."

"Yes, good observation, Maggie," she said. "But for next time. I'm just getting started, you know, and I wanted to paint the idyllic scene. Then I will expose some rottenness in Denmark."

Maggie thought it was pretty rotten to go entirely without the horses, but she kept it to herself.

"What do you think, Alma?" Nana asked.

"I . . . think you're catching your stride, Miz Hamilton. Sounds to me like you were born to it."

Nana smiled, just a little dimple indent, and folded the column's pages in thirds to tuck into the waiting envelope.

In the afternoon, Maggie sat at the kitchen table with two large bowls in front of her. Alma worked at the counter by the sink, humming cheerfully, not seeming to care if the weather was dreary, even acting friendly with the wood stove because she commented that it made the kitchen warm and cozy on a dark day.

Maggie took a fresh green bean from the bowl on her right, snapped off one end, pulled the string off the edge of the bean, then snapped off the bottom end. "Is this enough, Alma?" she asked with a sigh.

Alma peered into Maggie's bowl to see a huddle of seven or eight beans.

"For one person, maybe. Keep goin'."

Alma prepared a test batch of Mushroom Rollups for bridge club tomorrow. She brushed the tops of the prepared rollups with egg white, sprinkled them lightly with onion salt, cut them into half-inch slices, and slipped the slices on a cookie sheet into the oven to bake, promising Maggie goodness in about 20 minutes—give or take.

Then she stood at the counter beating together butter and sugar with a wooden spoon in a large mixing bowl for a batch of Wolferman's Chocolate Drop Cookies. Alma held the bowl against her bosom in the crook of her strong left arm and whipped the butter with the strength of a prizefighter.

"Hope you never have to spank me with that spoon, the way you're whippin' it around," Maggie said.

"You get a spankin', t'wouldn't be from me," Alma flashed her a grin of gleaming, even teeth. "Besides, you're too big a girl for that."

"I know. And I didn't get many, My mother would rather go in her room and ignore me when she's mad. But what about your children? Do you give them spankings?"

"What makes you think I have children?" asked Alma.

"I know you're married to Baxter. And you love to hold children in your lap."

"That's so. But the good Lord hasn't seen fit to give me any children. 'Cept you, of course."

"Does that make you sad?"

Alma stopped stirring and pressed her hand up against her nose. Tears pooled in her eyes, but she sniffed and lifted her head so they wouldn't run out.

"You're just about enough for one woman, Miss Maggie."

"You mean two women. Three with Nana," Maggie laughed. "But now my mother is all about the baby. You'd think she'd figure out that getting pregnant just makes her sick, and she should just be thankful that she's got me."

"Yes, maybe that's so."

"But isn't your husband sad not to have children? He doesn't even have me."

"Baxter and I have lots of family—nieces and nephews. He's gone a lot. I'd imagine he finds a child or two each trip who needs a little special attention."

"But it's not the same, is it?"

Alma whipped several beats, paused, then whipped again, in the space before she answered.

"I guess you don't know, Maggie, 'til you've tried it both ways."

Rain continued through the evening. It drummed on the roof and dripped from the eaves with great monotony. Even Max stayed home by the fire, which Grandpa poked and prodded about every half hour, adding logs as needed from the pile beside the hearth.

Each of them had assumed the place on a chair or the davenport that had become their territory, with their favorite configurations of throw pillow, blanket or footstool. Grandpa sat in the commodious armchair under a reading lamp and read *The New Yorker*. Smoke wafted above him as he absently worked his pipe, and above Max, who dangled a cigarette from his fingers.

From time to time Max, from the davenport, read aloud bits from *Life* magazine, like "'What did the US get for the $40 million given to Aviator Howard Hughes to build airplanes during the war?'" with photos of Hughes' expensive women and pastimes.

Maggie played Solitaire at the card table in back of the davenport with a rhythmic flick flick flick thud, flick flick flick thud. Having grown tired of losing at double Solitaire, Alma read a copy of *Vogue* on the other side of the card table.

"Whatchu reading?" Maggie asked, glancing across.

"I'm lookin' at the fashions I'll see in Topeka maybe five years from now," Alma licked her index finger and used it to turn the magazine page.

Sitting on the davenport next to Max, Nana reinforced her cross-word puzzle by putting a magazine behind it, and ticked the pencil eraser against her lips as she studied number 30 across. "What is a logical country for babies?" she asked no one in particular, although everyone knew she could solve these on her own, and that she was probably quizzing Maggie.

"How many letters?" asked Maggie.

"Seven."

Maggie continued flipping cards. The others read.

"Denmark," Grandpa mumbled around his pipe.

"Babies in Denmark? Much too cold!" said Nana.

"Bermuda," ventured Max. Maggie looked at the back of Uncle Max's head and noticed his red hair had a sticking up place that he must have missed with his comb.

"Nope."

"I know: Hungary!" blurted Maggie.

Grandpa chortled.

"No."

"But it's perfect!" cried Maggie.

"The word is Lapland."

They groaned.

"But Lapland isn't a country," volunteered Alma, as she turned a magazine page.

Nana studied Alma, then returned to her puzzle.

"Hey, Pops. Here's one for the paper," said Max, holding out the magazine to him. "Look. It's about wheat rustling. Wheat's selling for over two dollars a bushel, so this farmer has posted a guy with a rifle on top of his mountain of grain until he can get it to market."

"Ha! Makes me homesick," said Grandpa. He flipped through the magazine a few pages.

"Did you see this, Max? A study of the effect of atomic bombs on the Bikini Atoll in the Pacific. They set off a test bomb there, and it made the lagoon and beaches so radioactive the inhabitants can't come back." He returned the magazine to Max.

Maggie peered over Max's shoulder to view the color photos of radioactive algae and fish.

"Amazing what can be done with the new color films," said Max.

"Do you prefer using color?" asked Nana.

"Sometimes, but I still like to develop my own black and white."

"Did you know, Max, that one of the doors under the cabin leads to a darkroom?" Nana asked.

"You're kidding."

"The previous owner was an amateur photographer. We've never used it."

"Swell! I sure will!" Max crossed his feet in front of him and flicked open the magazine exuberantly.

Nana called out questions to complete her crossword puzzle. Maggie knew she was an everyday crossword worker, the kind who completes them and kicks herself if she has to peek at the answers. Herself an avid problem-solver, but an impatient crossword worker who frequently turned to the answer in the back, Maggie pulled the dictionary from the bookshelf under the window, getting ready.

"A taxi with one passenger," Nana asked.

Max said, "Cabriolet."

"Only children are so cooked."

"Coddled," ventured Grandpa.

"Capital is definitely below par now. Ends with 's'" Grandpa correctly guessed "Paris."

"Grading to make it cheap," Nana continued. "Seven letters. Ends with a 'd'."

"'Niggard', probably," said Grandpa.

"But I thought 'nigger' was a bad word," said Maggie.

"Not 'nigger,' Maggie. The word is 'niggard'," Nana clarified.

"But wouldn't they be alike?" Maggie thumbed through the dictionary and found it.

"A ha! 'Niggard' is of Scandinavian origin," Maggie read, "and means a miser: a covetous and stingy person. Whereas nigger is . . . is . . . "

No one came to Maggie's aid. Across the card table from her,

Alma studied a picture of a red-headed woman in a pink hat with a feather that curled over her head from earlobe to earlobe. Alma looked at Maggie, with eyes like hard, dark marbles, and did not offer an answer.

"'Nigger' is a Negro person 'graded to make them cheap,'" Maggie concluded.

Alma had returned to the curling pink hat in *Vogue*, but she looked at Maggie with eyes that were chocolate brown again, raised her chin, pursed up her lips, and gave her a nod.

Sailboat Race

ALTHOUGH THE SAILBOAT racing Regatta had gone on all week, Max seemed in no rush to enter a more strenuous, commitment-driven phase of his vacation. He gave the excuse that their sailboat wasn't yet in the water. But he got up on Thursday morning, while it was still morning, seemingly with a bee in his bonnet to get their decrepit E-scow, the The Dame, out from its canvas cover, her mast upright, her sails rigged, and her out in competition.

When Max gathered a pail, a scrub brush and sponges from Alma after breakfast, he asked her if she would help him, but she pointed to Nana's list on which she had circled "Bridge Club at 2:00 p.m." and said, "No, sir."

"Maggie, you'll help Uncle Max, won't you?" he asked.

"Sure, if I can crew for you."

"I'm covered at this point. I've got Susan and Teensy and a guy named Dave I met at the Pine Cone who says he's sailed. But if I need a fifth, you're on, Maggs," he said. So he included her in the process of preparing to race, which was after all nearly as fun as actually racing, what with the expectation that she *might* race and all. Besides, Maggie was hoping that Jamie and Bebo would see her

94

involved, scrubbing the sleek deck.

"Susan and Teensy aren't helping," Maggie said, as she began to tire of her task.

"Your powers of observation are brilliant, Nancy Drew," said Max as he squeezed a sponge into the lake. He said it too loud, like he wanted the girls on the dock nextdoor to hear, so Maggie shut up.

But the The Dame left the dock with a crew of four, barely in time to get to the starting line. Maggie watched from the dock as they launched out onto the lake, the crew awkwardly jockeyed for their positions on the boat, with Uncle Max telling them what to do. Maggie noticed that Teensy had been assigned the ballast, or dead weight position in the center of the boat, which probably didn't go over great with her. The Dame looked down-at-the-heels, even though Maggie'd scrubbed her hard. Her canvas sails were yellow and stained, and the wood on her hull begged for varnish.

Since Uncle Max's boat was a tippy scow, and she was sure he wasn't a good sailor, Maggie figured she'd just wait until she got an offer to crew on a better boat. Still, it stung a little that he didn't take her. Figured.

This year the fleet of E-scows had swelled with the addition of trophy boats. That's what Grandpa called it when fathers gave fancy new sailboats to their sons who had returned from the war. So Uncle Max was out-classed on two counts. Maggie knew with the crew he had, he would lose. Still, Maggie figured she would root for them, for boat E-19.

When the bridge ladies arrived, Alma was arranging perfect Mushroom Rollups prettily on a china plate. She had prepared tea in the silver teapot, and Maggie played with the tiny silver pinchers the ladies would use to grasp sugar cubes for their tea.

The last time Maggie looked, a dozen sailboats bobbed in a lethargic huddle without so much as a breeze to flutter their sails or spread apart the fast ones from the slow ones, the adept sailors from the lazy sometimes-sailors. Of which Uncle Max was one.

From the kitchen Maggie heard the wind rushing through the pine forests moments before the kitchen windows rattled and the porch door slammed shut. Nana burst through the swinging door to the kitchen as Alma tugged the window over the sink to close it.

"Come on, Maggie. Max might be over," Nana's eyebrows knit together, and the fright in her face got Maggie off her stool. Nana was never frightened.

"Since Frank's off fishing, we'll have to run rescue boat," Nana said. It looked like Maggie would be crew after all. She'd ride in the Chris Craft and fish them out of the drink. Then Uncle Max would see what she could do.

The bridge women stood at the porch screens, passing binoculars back and forth. Maggie stood in the line-up, and grabbed hold of the binoculars as they were passed above her head, to take a turn.

"Will any of you ladies be driving rescue boats?" Maggie asked.

"Good heavens, Maggie!" Nana chided.

The three women seemed to notice her for the first time.

"Our youngest son will cover it," said Tilly Wyatt, "though Jeffrey generally doesn't need a rescue."

"We don't sail, Maggie, the doctor . . ." Mrs. Gerrard said, watching the boats and not saying more.

Mrs. Haggerty laughed her sharp, high little laugh.

"Looks like there's just one tipped over," said Mrs. Gerrard, when the binoculars came her way. "No . . . two. Five!"

"What's Max's number?" Nana asked Maggie as she took her turn with the binoculars.

"E-19. Do you see it?"

Nana didn't reply, and looked at Maggie as if she'd swallowed a frog. She passed off the binoculars, and quickly gathered jackets, rain slickers, and a pile of beach towels from hooks and shelves by the porch door. Maggie silently helped her, and they dashed down the steps to the lake.

In the boathouse, as Maggie slipped her arms through an orange life vest and Nana untied the painter that secured the Chris Craft, Alma appeared in the doorway. She wore her white having-company uniform with one of Grandpa's plaid jackets and an oilcloth tablecloth wrapped around her for a raincoat. A pair of Uncle Max's sunglasses gave the outfit a movie star tilt.

"I don't do boats," she said, and she did look like she could only do a substantial boat, "but you need help."

Nana nodded, and while she revved the boat engine, Alma stepped onto the back seat, and lowered herself into the boat. Maggie slipped into the front passenger seat.

Nana backed the boat out into a churning, white-capped lake. The rain had not yet come, but its escort, the east wind, skimmed water from the lake's roiling surface and flung it at the Chris Craft in sheets, drenching them.

Behind Mt. Baldy, dark clouds amassed and began their assault. Forks of lightning jabbed from the dark billows, each seeming closer to the lake. Maggie knew from her aptitude in science and from her finely-tuned intuition that it would not be good to be caught sitting under a sailboat's mast if lightning struck the lake. Nor would it be wise to be sitting in a Chris Craft, but the three women continued to the rescue with all the speed that the tossing waves allowed them.

"Can you swim?" Nana yelled to Alma.

"I don't think so."

By the time the Chris Craft traversed the lake, the number of sailboats overturned was greater than the number upright. The ones that stayed top-up flew with the wind, all crew perched on the high side of the boat and leaning out to extend their weight. Maggie couldn't imagine Teensy doing this, so perhaps it was just as well they had gotten it over with quickly.

Nana idled the Chris Craft as they neared the The Dame, lying on its side in the water. She circled it at a distance of several yards to keep clear of the sails and rigging, visible just under the surface, and to find all four sailors, who hung onto the boat as best they could, bobbing and gasping in the cold mountain stream-fed lake. Maggie easily distinguished the two girls by their clinging wet blouses.

"Mother!" bellowed Max. "It's about time. Where were you?"

"Playing bridge, Maxwell. Perhaps I should have stayed there."

Nana sat with her bottom on the top of the seat, so that she leaned well above the steering wheel and could see above the water-splattered windshield.

"You're supposed to be out watching!" Max was mad, but couldn't convey it well because his teeth chattered.

"Shall we just get on with this, Max?" Nana yelled over the wind.

The two girls didn't wait to see what would happen, but sidestroked over to the Chris Craft, and Alma helped pull them into the back of the motorboat. Then she mummied them in beach towels and they huddled low from the wind in the backseat. Alma hugged them on either side of her like she was protecting baby chicks.

Nana idled the tossing Chris Craft near the tip of the mast, which was visible about a foot under water. But as she drew near, the wind jostled the motorboat away, just out of reach of it. Nana circled the sailboat and came at it again, but this added the Chris' wake to the mess of churning waves surrounding the sailboat.

While Nana jockeyed to get the motorboat in position within reach of the tip of the mast, Max dog-paddled in the water, loosening the halyard from the mast and then tugging the big sail down. This made sense to Maggie, to minimize the resistance of this expanse of canvas when they tried to get the boat aright.

Maggie tried to help by explaining to Max how he could do it more quickly, but he told her to shut up and fumbled along. Finally he was able to tug the sail down perhaps six feet from the tip of the mast, which now peeked above the surface.

"Alma, grab it! Grab the end of the mast!" Max yelled.

Alma struggled to get up from the back seat of the boat, and the two huddled girls got out of her way. She leaned over the side of the boat, grasped the mast tip from the water, and as she did so she tilted her side of the Chris Craft to within licking distance of the breaking waves. Seeming to know without asking what she must do, Alma grasped the mast in both hands and heaved it up, up, up. Up more as she got to her feet on the backseat cushion. Up again as Alma balanced one foot on the motor box and continued to lift it. Meanwhile the Chris Craft rocked crazily, so that the upheld mast danced, pointing skyward at about 2:10. The mast rose higher and Alma walked it up with her hands. She looked like a great black-and-white statue of a sailboat Iwo Jima.

The sailboat groaned as its wooden deck tilted toward level again. Max had swum around the sailboat so he could pull himself onto it as soon as it hit the water upright. Crew Member Dave had been hanging onto the upturned bottom of the boat all along, so he was ready to dive onto the sailboat when it righted.

Alma held the mast up as high as she could, and the two boys pulled on the boat's high side, but it didn't seem quite enough. Maggie knew if she lent her hand it would make Alma's efforts victorious. So she climbed into the back of the boat and braced herself against Alma, reaching upward. . . .

After dinner, Nana had a headache and prepared for bed early. She stood in her flannel robe and felt slippers toasting her backside by the fire. Maggie pretended to be reading at the card table, hoping to remove herself from the conversation.

"Maggie, what on earth were you thinking?" Nana was really mad.

Grandpa peered at Nana over his magazine, pipe in his hand.

"But Janie, she was just trying to help. Aren't you being a little hard on her?"

"Alma could have drowned! And Maggie too—in water a hundred feet deep!" The fire's heat was warming more than Nana' backside.

"How would you like to have a gallery of motorboats watching as your son screamed at you? Or watch four volunteer firemen haul your maid and your granddaughter into the tourist motor launch using float rings, hooks and ropes? I tell you, Frank, it was just . . . too . . . much." Nana rubbed her forehead. "Now Alma's out in her room tossing and moaning.

"I had Maggie take soup and a sandwich to her, and when I asked Maggie how she was, she said 'lamenting.'"

"Was that Alma's word or Maggie's?" Grandpa asked.

"Oh, never mind," Nana said, shaking a hand at him.

Before Nana had toasted enough and had gone up to bed, Max returned from the Pine Cone Inn uncharacteristically early. They heard him rummaging in the kitchen, and then he came through the living room on his way to the stairs, holding a lumpy tea towel against his right eye.

"Max, come here. What happened to you?" Nana asked.

He paused half-way up the stairs. "Nothing." He stopped again, then said, "Susan and Teensy were playing up to a volunteer fireman at the Pine Cone. Guy said he'd done his share of water rescues, but the dolphin act with the colored woman and the kid was a new one for him. I showed him that I didn't think that was funny. I didn't care that he was a war vet." He continued up the stairs and Grandpa looked at Nana with a well-how-do-you-like-that expression. She followed Max up the stairs.

After Nana went up to bed, Maggie decided to go out and check on Alma one more time. She found her lying in bed with one arm over her eyes, moaning softly as Mahalia Jackson lamented from a phonograph record.

I'm on my way to Canaan land. I'm on my way, Glory Hallelujah, I'm on my way. I had a mighty hard time, but I'm on my way. I had a mighty hard time, but I'm on my way.

She had pulled an extra blanket over the bedspread, even though the heater on the wall pinged and popped and the place was stiflingly hot. She acknowledged Maggie's presence by reaching out her hand to touch Maggie's.

The dinner Maggie had brought to her sat uneaten on the small desk in the corner. Velvetta leaked from the grilled cheese sandwich into a greasy yellow pool. Scum coated the surface of the bowl of tomato soup. In a framed print above the desk, two Hummel figures skipped down a road arm in arm.

Under the desk lamp, two postcards were propped on the top shelf of the desk, between an opened bag of bridge mix and Alma's limp rabbit's foot. Figuring anyone who wrote postcards must expect them to be read by anyone, Maggie read them for any clues they may provide to Alma's true condition.

Both pictured Grand Lake in sunset splendor. On one, Alma had marked an X on the spot of this afternoon's water rescue. On the writing side, the compressed handwriting was barely legible.

Thursday, August 14, 1947
Dear Mama,

I nearly sank to the depths. I was hauled into a boat like a side of pork at the market. We're half way through our time here, and I'm about even with the wood stove. I don't burn things any more, but neither do I have my magic. Maybe I should have come visit you like I planned. But one thing you wouldn't believe. Today your girl was swimming! If that was swimming.

Your Loving Daughter,
Alma

The second postcard propped on the desk lacked the X. Inside Alma had written:

Thursday, August 14, 1947
Dear Baxter,

Fishing in the streams is pretty good here. Folks are catching brown trout, brook trout, and rainbows. You will not believe this, but I swam in the lake today. I've got my hands full with Mr. Max and Miss Maggie, so it's a good thing they brought me along, although I miss you mightily.

What are you finding to do at home? Are you at home?

I would love to hear from you, Baby, just a card. It would mean so much to me.

Your Loving Wife,
Alma

Maggie replaced the postcards and stood by Alma's bed, touching her strong arm lying on top of the blanket. "You all right, Alma?"

Alma left her other arm over her eyes and licked her lips as though they were wanting for saliva, then said, "Course, Miss Maggie. Takes more 'n' that to keep Alma down."

"I didn't mean to hurt you, Alma."

"Shhhhh. I know it, Baby Girl. You go on now, ya hear?"

"You get some sleep. See you in the morning, Alma." Maggie patted her arm and left.

Dear Diary Thursday, August 14, 1947

Any doubt as to my qualifications to solve mysteries was put to rest in a daring double rescue today, although unfortunately my grandparents aren't looking at it that way.

The first rescue involved Uncle Max's sailboat capsizing in high seas with an incompetent crew. To right the boat, when it was obvious that Alma would not be able to hoist the tip of the mast high enough, I jumped nimbly onto her back and flung it from her hands, providing the needed final boost.

Even Nancy Drew could not, I am confident, have accomplished this feat. Granted I was not wearing a dress, and I did have the advantage of a life preserver, which I donned on accurate premonition. But in none of the mysteries I have read to date has Nancy rescued a 200-pound woman with no life preserver who doesn't swim and is thrashing and screaming.

Knowing that the Showboat most certainly kept devices aboard for a water rescue, I swam a strong sidestroke up to it, asked their further assistance, and sent a watching motorboat for volunteer firemen. This course of action I embarked upon as I saw the Showboat to be half full of huddled little old ladies, and so it would obviously be of no help whatsoever in hauling Alma to safety.

Keeping my wits about me, I removed Alma's sunglasses while she clung to me to keep from sinking. Then I guided the life ring over Alma's head to provide flotation, because my life jacket was not enough for both of us.

All of this is well and good, but I'm not telling Nana about what my mother said about polio in the letter I got today. I guess the swimming pool in Topeka is closed and kids are hardly allowed to play with their friends. So, can I get polio from swimming in Grand Lake? From taking in gulps of lake water while trying to save a Hannah Gruen who can't swim? I will do some more research about that.

The sad part is that Alma has not recovered yet from her near-drowning. She is not her perky self, I'll tell you that. Nana, Grandpa, Uncle Max, and I fixed our own grilled cheese sandwiches for dinner tonight while Alma recovered in her cabin. I took dinner out to her and she was in bed, generally limp. I hope she'll get well in the night and be back in the kitchen tomorrow and realize that she has an exciting adventure to share with her children, which someday she may have.

Sincerely,

Maggie the Unsinkable

Battling Boredom

Who should Maggie find standing at the wood stove the next morning but Nana, with one of Alma's big aprons wound around her twice, stirring a stiff blob of oatmeal that followed the spoon around the pan.

At her place at the table Maggie found two pieces of toast and some orange juice.

"Good Morning, Maggie," Nana said. "Sorry about the oatmeal, but the stove is a challenge, I will say." She plopped a portion into a bowl and set it in front of Maggie, who doused it with milk, dusted it with brown sugar, and stirred it well.

"Where's Alma?"

Nana passed a note across the table.

Dear Mrs. Hamilton,

I will be taking some time to recuperate this morning, but will be in for my morning chores. I hope this will not inconvenience you.

Yours Sincerely,
Alma

"I guess Alma deserves a break," said Nana. "I was so worried about her. I wish you had just let it be, Maggie. She was so close to raising the mast. She was so brave."

Tears stung Maggie's eyes, and to hide them she doctored her oatmeal some more. If only Nana could see that she was the bravest one. What about her courageous water rescue?

"But I didn't know that, Nana. And I saved her from drowning." Maggie fought to control little quivers in her voice.

"Yes, you did, but I wish to heaven she hadn't gone in." Nana turned to the sink to run water into the oatmeal pan.

Maggie excused herself quickly after eating a decent show of oatmeal, and went to her room, trying to keep her legs from running. She snuggled back in her unmade bed with her clothes on and watched rivulets of rain streak down her window, wondering what her mother and daddy were doing at home, and if they were thinking of her, or maybe starting to forget her. After a while she picked up her book, but a tolling bell in a watery cave did not rouse her interest.

Mid-morning Maggie wandered downstairs and found Alma flicking around the feather duster in the living room, but not humming.

"I'm sorry that I made you fall in the lake yesterday, Alma."

"You know, Miss Maggie," Alma said, dropping her duster to her side, "you might need to sort out when you do, and when you do not need to save the day. Sometimes other folks have things well in hand themselves."

"One more thing, then I believe we can put this episode to rest. I don't want you to go telling nobody about it, ya hear?" Alma poked her duster at Maggie and looked at her wide-eyed, as if she'd know it, even from beyond the grave, if Maggie ever did.

"Okay, Alma. Do you still love me?"

Maggie's eyes looked large and green and not as sure of things as usual. So Alma sat down on the davenport and pulled Maggie onto her lap for a big hug. Which led to giggles, and guffaws, chortles and *tee hee hees*.

"You looked so funny, Alma."

"But I was swimmin' girl—wasn't I? Huh?"

As Alma got up and back to work, Maggie threw a blanket over herself on the davenport. "It's a gloomy ole day," she said.

"Again!" said Alma.

"Where is everybody?" Maggie asked.

"Your grandmother's taking a tour of the water pumping plant. Research for her next newspaper column. Mr. Max is over next door, and Mr. Hamilton had a meeting this morning." Alma had traded the feather duster for a rag to wipe the tables and chair arms.

"I have an idea," Alma turned to Maggie, flicking out her dust cloth. She went to the phonograph player next to the bookcase and inspected the album jackets until she found what she wanted. She carefully dusted the platter before putting it on the turntable, then started the phonograph player and gently placed the needle arm down at the outer edge of the record. Bing Crosby crooned "The Whiffenpoof Song."

We're poor little lambs that have lost our way. Ba ba ba.

Alma held the duster like a microphone and crooned as Maggie giggled,

We're little black sheep who have gone astray. Ba ba ba.

As the song ended and the phonograph needle cycled out of the alley between songs and into the next one, Maggie jumped up and grabbed the needle arm, running a scratch with a zipping noise across the Whiffenpoofs as she tried to play it again. Sure enough, the needle stuck at the scratch, repeating the same phrase over and over.

"Why did I know you were going to do that?" Alma asked, raising her eyes heavenward. "Now what are you going to tell your Uncle Max?"

"What are *you* going to tell Uncle Max?" Maggie smart-mouthed to Alma, not because she was mad at her, but because she was mad at herself. "You're the one who was playing his record."

"Miss Maggie, you march right up to your room! You're not going to talk to me thata way." As Maggie left, Alma slowly raised the phonograph arm, removed Bing from the spindle, and dusted him with the feather duster. Then she slipped the record into its white paper undershirt, and slipped the undershirt into its jacket, and slipped the jacket into the center of Uncle Max's record collection.

Maggie threw her body across her bed and fumed awhile. Her mother often said that she got into trouble when she was bored. And she was bored. What would un-bored her was finding clues to solve her mystery. The thought flickered across her mind that she didn't know whether Nana owned a squashed blossom necklace. Maybe Grandpa bought one for her up here some summers ago.

Maggie snuck into her grandparents' bedroom, which smelled of Brylcreem and Nana's Chanel #5. In the corner by the window, Nana's small dressing table was skirted around with blue-and-white checked gingham fabric to hide the contents of the lower shelves. An oval mirror hung above the table.

Maggie sat gingerly on the vanity stool. She steeled herself from taking a squirt of perfume from the tiny glass perfume bottle on the table, since this would be a dead give away of where she'd been. She picked up Nana's silver-topped hairbrush, running her finger over the silver swirls on the back of the brush. Then she pulled the rubber bands out of her pigtails and brushed her auburn hair, which Maggie thought was her best feature. It was thick and wavy, flecked with gold strands, and touched her shoulders, this being as long as her mother allowed her to grow it. Since it's impossible to see your best features without also seeing your blemishes, Maggie peered into the mirror at a tiny dent in her forehead where her mother had accidentally jabbed her with the point of the scissors while cutting her bangs. And she attempted to see herself in profile to determine if her nose was getting too big yet.

Maggie left her hair loose to look elegant for trying on Nana's Indian jewelry. Downstairs she could hear Alma running the Electrolux in the living room.

She carefully pulled back the gingham drape to reveal a shelf of jars and tubes of creams and cosmetics, but on a second shelf Maggie found the mahogany jewelry box in which Nana kept her long strand of pearls and her ruby and diamond earrings.

The jewelry box, which Maggie set on top of the dressing table, had three compartments: one inside the top lid, and two pull-out drawers. Maggie loved compartments and relished the search. The two drawers held treasures in silver and turquoise, but no squash blossom necklace.

First Maggie fished out a long silver barrette inlaid with small round turquoise stones. The striations and flecks of dark in the stones made them each unique and interesting, just as the Old Maid sales lady had said.

Using Nana's comb, Maggie parted her hair on one side. She brushed it smooth and clasped the barrette to hold a swoosh of hair over one eyebrow.

Then Maggie pulled out several silver bracelets, some just curved silver bands, some with inlaid designs and turquoise stones. She lined up four on her left wrist and three on her right, pressing the ends together to bend the silver to better fit her wrists.

She peered into the mirror, chin high, with her hands clasped under her chin so that the bracelets showed up and down her arms.

The vacuum whined, but Maggie caught movement in the corner of her eye.

"Playing dress up?"

Maggie reeled around to face Nana standing at the foot of the bed. Fortunately Maggie had learned that when you're caught red-handed, the truth is usually the slickest way out of a predicament.

"I . . . didn't know whether you had a squashed blossom necklace,

Nana. I didn't think you'd mind if I found out, and you weren't here to ask."

As Nana approached her at the dressing table, Maggie cowered, waiting. To her surprise, Nana removed the silver barrette, smoothed Maggie's hair with the brush, and re-clipped it. Then she kept brushing the back of Maggie's hair as she talked. "Did you know you look so like your mother at your age?

"You must be bored on these rainy days. I have an idea. But first you must put all the jewelry back carefully, just as I had it. Let's test your powers of observation."

Nana left the room and Maggie confidently put each piece back in the compartment where she found it. Leaving her hair brushed and down, Maggie gave herself a farewell look in Nana's mirror. At the very least, the day was getting more interesting.

When Maggie got downstairs, Nana was calling someone on the wall telephone in the dining room.

"Hello, Louise? It's Jane. Hope I'm not disturbing you."

Maggie sat on a dining room chair and listened, since Nana didn't wave her away.

"Yes, it is a lot of rain. Setting records, I hear, although Edgar says the town only started keeping rain and snowfall records recently."

"Yes, well, I have a favor to ask of you. Would it be too much trouble—Could I bring Maggie over to talk with you about your squash blossom necklace? Yes, I know this is unusual."

"—But perhaps she can help you, Louise. It couldn't hurt, could it? I mean, you do want to find it."

"No, of course I would stay with her."

"No, I haven't talked to anyone outside of bridge club."

"Well, I certainly didn't mean to distress you. We've been friends for many years, and you should know—"

"Oh!"

"Well!"

"I'm sorry that's the way you feel about it."

"Good-bye."

Nana stared ahead. Then her vision focused upon Maggie. "Mrs. Haggerty thinks we are meddling in her affairs. I cannot take you over there. And she is resigning from bridge club, since her personal affairs are not safe to discuss there."

"I'm sorry, Nana. I only meant to help."

"I know, dear. But I'm in quite a mess now. I wonder if Tilly and Norma will still want to play."

In the past two days Maggie had seen two new emotions from her grandmother: Nana frightened, and now, Nana sad. Both upset Maggie, and she wished she could do something.

Nana sighed and rose from the chair. "I think I'll go up and take a hot bath."

Maggie sat chewing on a ragged fingernail and grieving the trouble she had made for Nana, and the loss of her first real mystery, without which she did not want to think about another half-month's vacation. Especially a rainy one.

"*Alllmmmmmmmma!*" Nana wailed from upstairs.

14

Running Muck

ALMA PULLED ON the stair railing to help propel herself upward with such amazing haste that Maggie assumed Alma had also never heard such a call of distress from Nana's lips.

Nana stood in the bathroom in her flannel bathrobe with her hair in pin curls. But the water running from the faucet into the white enamel bathtub was brackish, not clear. And worse, slime oozed up from the bathtub drain.

"Alma, what is that?" Nana asked, pointing.

"Looks to me like the drain's backed up," said Alma. She tried the water in the sink, and it also ran dirty. The toilet water was dingy too.

"Can you fix it?" Nana asked.

"No, ma'am."

Nana cinched the ties on her bathrobe.

"Nana, I'll get to the bottom of this for you," Maggie volunteered.

"Maggie, this is just about all I can handle without that!" Nana said. "Let's see if this town has a plumber."

While Nana dressed, Alma put stoppers in the drains throughout the house, which now smelled like the latrine at summer camp.

Nana's first telephone call was to the local plumber, who did not answer, but Maybelle, the telephone operator, informed Nana that he must be out on a job and that nearly all the incoming calls were for him.

Then Nana called her bridge group, except Louise Haggerty, to discover that the Gerrards were affected, but the Wyatts were not. From what they pieced together, by who had heard what, the problem seemed to be localized to homes and businesses at the end of the lake closest to the channel to Shadow Mountain Reservoir.

Swinging into high gear, Nana sent Alma and Maggie to town in the Gray Gazelle to purchase buckets and large containers for hauling water, but there were none available because local restaurants and tourist cottages had beaten them to the punch. At Maggie's suggestion they even checked at Rustic Stables, where they were assured that they needed all the buckets that they had.

That day vacation became a series of challenges to take care of their most basic bodily functions. When they finally reached him by telephone, the plumber said it was an Act of God and out of his control, and they just had to wait until things settled out.

They took what Nana called birdie baths from the sink at the Wyatts, and Alma prepared meals there for the Hamiltons, the Gerrards, and the Wyatts. They ate in shifts because the cabin was small, and the rains continued.

To Maggie's delight, Jamie and Bebo and she spent hours together playing Hearts or Gin Rummy at the Wyatt's cabin. Dr. Gerrard had made the unfortunate choice of this as a weekend to visit his family at the lake, so Maggie saw the chance to do some research.

"Mr. Gerrard," Maggie approached him as he sat reading a newspaper.

"Doctor Gerrard," Jamie whispered.

"Dr. Gerrard," Maggie restarted, struggling to keep her gaze on his light blue eyes rather than his fakey foot sticking into his shoe. "I have a question about polio."

Jamie groaned.

"Polio is hardly a vacation topic, Maggie," laughed Dr. Gerrard.

"That's what I thought, but my mother says they've shut down the swimming pool at home, and I'm wondering if you can get polio from swimming in the lake. Say, swimming and getting a mouthful of water."

At such times Maggie was thankful to wear glasses, because they made her look smarter, as if her eyes had been strained from extra brain effort.

"Hmmm. I would think that only a remote possibility, Maggie, given the size of this body of water and how cold it is."

Maggie thanked him. At least now she knew there was no reason for her mother to worry Nana that maybe Maggie's legs would be paralyzed from swimming in the lake.

On Monday morning, Grandpa assured Nana that he shared her distress that the cabin had been defiled, but that there was nothing he could do at present, so that he might as well go fishing and keep out of her way. He promised her a fish fry at the woodpile that evening if the weather cleared.

That morning the telephone rang, and Nana answered.

"Yes, quite a mess, I can tell you."

"That's a relief. I'm happy for you."

"Oh? Thank you, but we wouldn't think of inconveniencing you."

"Good-bye."

"Who was that?" Maggie asked as Nana passed through the living room on her way upstairs. She wouldn't have asked, but Nana looked jangled.

"It was Louise Haggerty, Maggie. She offered her home if we needed it."

Maggie sucked in her breath.

"But of course that's out of the question."

"But Nana—"

Maggie got the turtle eye, so she punched the sofa pillow. Rats! Why did she find such a stupid mystery? She wished she could just forget all about it, but not as much as she wished that she could solve it.

Later that morning, Nana sent Maggie to the post office to get the mail, where she overheard the postmistress tell a patron that the State Board of Health had condemned the town's wells and summer water supply, putting some of the resorts out of business for the rest of the season. When Maggie reported this news back at the cabin, Nana sniffed, then continued knitting at a pace that Maggie feared would cause sparks in the wool. Eventually she stuck the needles into the baby blanket and stood up. "Maggie, we're going to town. I believe it's time we meet the mayor and see what they're doing about this."

Wearing her fringed leather jacket, Maggie waited in the kitchen talking to Alma, who had dark circles under her eyes from doing her daily battle using Pine Sol, plus cooking for a crowd each night. From the commotion upstairs, they determined that Nana had roused Max from bed, because she wanted him to go along. What on earth for?

Nana led the entourage into Jimmy's Cafe, because Jimmy was the mayor and owned the establishment. Nana was dressed city-ish in a skirt and blouse with a sweater draped around her shoulders, and Maggie thought she looked handsome.

Jimmy's Café was filling with the lunchtime crowd. The waitress summoned the mayor, and as he came out of the kitchen he removed his white apron and with a quick maneuver of his hands around his belt made sure that his shirttail was tucked in. He was a short man with bushy eyebrows and a handlebar mustache, and seemed to count on the power of hair.

"You must be the mayor?" Nana said.

"Yes, I'm Jim Jacobs."

"I'm Jane Hamilton," she said, extending her right hand. "I'm a summer resident, and also a member of the press, and I would like to interview you about this calamity."

Nana introduced him to the rest of them and he shepherded them to a small table in the back corner of the restaurant, after whispering to the waitress, who brought them bottles of Coca Cola.

While he waited for Nana to speak, the mayor fidgeted with his left mustache handle.

"This is not what we had in mind on vacation, our first in four years, and I'm wondering what the town is doing about this, Mr. Jacobs."

"As a matter of fact, Mrs. Hamilton, you are the third person I've seen this morning. In the restaurant here our grease traps have backed up. You think *you* have a problem!"

"Is it true that the town water and septic systems have been condemned?" Nana asked.

"And why does this town have the creeping crud?" Maggie added, leaning forward and resting her fringed sleeves on the table.

"Some of the Old Timers think it's because of all the rainfall this summer," said the mayor. "Others swear that flooding Shadow Mountain Reservoir made the water table rise. At any rate, the wells have been compromised and the septic system leach fields are flooded."

"At the north and west ends of the lake?" Nana clarified.

"Yes, that seems to be the extent of it."

"The end of the lake that joins with the new reservoir?"

"Yes."

"So this would tend to substantiate the reservoir theory."

"One could look at it that way."

"If that is the reason, when will this get better, Mayor?"

"When the water level goes down, or the leach fields adapt and settle out."

"Oh. And when might that be?" Nana asked, rather dramatically for the occasion, Maggie thought, but still, she was impressive.

"Very soon, we hope, of course. Look, Mrs. Hamilton, what exactly can I do for you?"

"Answer one more question. What is the town doing about the presence of its raw sewage in the previously pristine waters of Grand Lake? I was fishing the other day, Mr. Jacobs, and a head of lettuce

115

floated past me. Pumping the reservoir waters through Grand Lake to the tunnel to Estes Park is one issue, Mr. Jacobs, beyond your jurisdiction, I know. But the sewage treatment issue, surely, rests with you." Nana sat back in her chair and looked at him as though she held all the good cards in her hand.

The mayor picked up the fork in front of him on the table and waved it as if he was going to use it as an exclamation point. "Well, Mrs. Hamilton, we are working on a plan for a new treatment facility to remedy that. . . ."

"Which leads me to the important question of polio, Mr. Mayor," Maggie said.

The mayor squirmed and looked at Nana as if hoping she might shush Maggie. But Nana waited.

"Polio is passed from being around poop and not washing your hands, Mr. Mayor, and just think of all the dirty hands around here right now. Alllll that dirty water." Maggie adopted Nana's cock of the head.

The mayor now looked at Max for help since Nana wasn't budging, but he was fiddling with his camera.

"As a matter of fact," said the mayor, puffing up in his chair, "we have a town council meeting scheduled for tomorrow night, to address these weighty matters. Why don't you check back with me after the meeting?"

"Better yet, we will have a representative *at* the meeting. It's open to the public, I trust? At least to the press?" Nana asked.

"Yes . . . of course."

"Mother," said Max, lifting his black camera, "would you please lean closer to the mayor for a photo?"

The mayor dabbed at his mustache handles with a napkin, even though he hadn't eaten anything. He pulled them into position and looked solemn for the camera, trying to sit up taller than Nana, but he couldn't.

Maggie tugged on Max's elbow when he had finished a series of

116

clicks. "What about me?" she asked.

"Sure, Maggs," Uncle Max winked at her, and Maggie stood between Nana and the mayor, attempting to look studious.

As they walked to the car, Nana looked at Maggie with a sideways smile. "What's this about polio, Maggie? What made you think of that?"

Maggie smiled and kept her sources to herself.

The heavens smiled with a dry, clean face that evening, so Alma toweled off the benches at the woodpile, and she fried fish on a grate over the wood fire. Nana, Grandpa, Maggie and the Professor sat on the pig benches viewing a glorious sunset. To be out of the smelly cabin on a clear summer evening lifted their spirits high. Grandpa was chipper and talking Poor Old Kansas talk. They did that a lot. "Thermometer reads 63 degrees here now; yesterday's *Gazette* said the Topeka temp hit 111."

After dinner Maggie got to pitch horseshoes with the adults, since they needed a fourth. Maggie and Grandpa were a team, and then Nana and the Professor, which must have given Nana fits. He'd obviously not combed his hair after taking off his fishing hat. Gray hairs stuck out in revolt on his head and on his stubbly chin. Maggie's pitches fell far short, or flew wild, so they let her pitch several paces closer to the posts. But they treated her like she was a real adult horseshoe pitcher.

Grandpa and the Professor bragged about their fly-fishing, and their Will-Rogers-rope-trick casting, and then Nana told them about her visit with the mayor, without mentioning the upcoming town meeting.

"In one way the problem's a blessing," said the Professor. "This town's needed a modern sewage treatment system for years, and they've ignored it, sending the sewage down the Colorado. Now this has forced the issue. But the bigger problem'll just get worse, unless

Congress decides to actually use the money to study water clarity in Grand Lake."

"Seems like the town's best chance to get the Bureau's attention, and Congress' attention, is right now, in this current predicament," Grandpa said, posed with a horseshoe.

The shoe struck the post true and swung around it in a victory dance.

"Right! We need your help," the Professor said.

"But I don't even live here!"

"You kidding? You do your best living here! Town meeting's scheduled for tomorrow night. We've got an attorney and a geologist. Now we need a writer to present our case for the Bureau so we don't sound like a bunch of small town yokels ranting about crap."

Maggie tossed a leaner up against the post, but Nana's next throw ringed Maggie's and trumped it.

"I told the mayor this morning that you would attend, Frank," Nana said.

"Janie, why did you do that?"

"Because I know you," she said, and Maggie was sure she saw Nana give a pat on the back of Grandpa's saggy britches as she passed him to pitch a shoe from the other side.

"This will cut seriously into my fishing time," said Grandpa, scowling.

"Look at it as an investment in next year's fishing time, and the next, and the next," the Professor said.

"I'm not interested in investments right now, Professor. I'm into vacation."

15

Company's Coming

MAGGIE AWOKE TO the fresh smell of pines that she remembered from the early days at the lake. And sure enough, a sign posted on the upstairs bathroom door read "Back in Operation."

The sewage had settled, the water ran clear, and the atmosphere in the house felt buoyant. Maggie found Alma sitting in the living room surveying her morning list, her feet propped on the footstool and her new black cowboy boots standing next to her chair.

"Good Morning, Alma. Going to wear your new cowboy boots today?" Maggie had been with Alma when she purchased the boots from their favorite sales lady at Thunderbird's. All the cowgirl boots had been too small for her.

"When my feet are ready."

"They're supposed to be 'the most comfortable footwear you've ever worn.'"

"Well, they aren't yet." Alma pointed her pencil at her flaming bunions.

"Anyway, from the looks of today's doings, it won't be the day for wearin' 'em in."

Maggie stood behind Alma's chair and read Nana's list over her shoulder. Alma held two pieces of paper joined with a paper clip. The top sheet was a letter addressed to Nana and written on powder blue monogrammed stationery.

MGJ

Estes Park, Colorado
August 18, 1947
Dear Jane,

George and I would like to take you up on your kind invitation of dinner and lodging during our Colorado vacation. We plan to drive over from Estes Park to Grand Lake on Friday, August 22nd, and stay until Sunday. Our daughter Helen with us, and I hope her addition won't inconvenience you. As you know, Helen will be a sophomore at Southern Methodist University and has pledged Kappa Kappa Gamma. She and Max met at your cabin when they were ten, and I'm sure she would love to renew their acquaintance if he is with you.

George wanted me to particularly ask, since I hear that Alma is helping you, that she prepare her Fresh Coconut Cake he is so fond of. If it's not too much trouble.

We'll see you on Friday before noon.

Fondly,
Martha

"That Fresh Coconut Cake you're reading about . . ." said Alma.

"It's my favorite," said Maggie.

"Of course it's your favorite. That cake's my masterpiece. A trial even in the Topeka oven, but I will rise to the occasion—if I'm not dead before Friday," by which Alma referred to the second page, her to-do list.

Written on a piece of newsprint, Nana's elegant handwriting flowed upstream in a way that Maggie knew would not have pleased her. Nana did better with lines.

"Seems your grandmother has planned a major cleaning offensive," said Alma, "with company comin' tomorrow."

Kawuneeche Cabin, Thursday, August 21, 1947
   Note: Be prepared to move Max from his bedroom on Friday morning and to prepare his room for Helen. He will stay in the bedroom on the side of the maid's cabin with its own entrance, so you must clean that room.

This note brought a rumble of laughter from Alma that she squelched behind her hand. "He will loooove that," she said.

CHORES FOR THURSDAY

THOROUGHLY CLEAN BATHROOMS AND KITCHEN

DUST DOWNSTAIRS

CHANGE BEDS AND TAKE SHEETS TO LAUN-DRO-MAT

CLEAN BEDROOM FOR MAX IN MAID'S CABIN

Alma had drawn a box around the menu for the day, as if herding the sloping letters back in line:

MENU

BREAKFAST: POACHED EGGS ON TOAST, RASPBERRIES, MILK
AND COFFEE

LUNCH (INCLUDING PICNIC FOR FRANK): CHICKEN SALAD
SANDWICHES, POTATO CHIPS, GREEN GRAPES, COKES

DINNER FOR 4 AT 6:00 P.M

ON THE PORCH, WEATHER PERMITTING

BAKED BRISKET OF BEEF

CHEESE GRITS

CARROTS WITH ORANGE

MONTE CARLO SQUARES

121

NOTE: I WILL WRITE MY COLUMN IN THE MORNING AND GO TO THE BEAUTY PARLOR IN THE AFTERNOON, SO PLEASE KEEP AN EYE ON MAGGIE.

"You don't need to keep an eye on me," said Maggie.

"No, I know I don't, because you're going to do something solid today, like go over to your friends' house or work a jigsaw puzzle with a thousand pieces."

When Nana sat down to the typewriter mid-morning, Maggie worked on the pirate puzzle, and Alma moved her dust cloth in a path around the living room.

Nana sat up lodge pole pine straight and typed with confident pressure to the keys, consulting her written outline from time to time.

"Alma," Nana said presently, without looking up from the keys, "will you please dust this typewriter for me? I don't see how Frank stands all this pipe tobacco down the crevices."

Alma applied a dampened rag to the keys, wedged it between them, and lifted the machine to clean under it, accidentally striking keys as she worked.

"Oh, I'm sorry, Miz Hamilton."

"It's all right, Alma," said Nana, but she ripped the page from the typewriter and cranked in a clean sheet with a sigh that indicated that Alma was forgiven, but clumsy.

When Nana finished typing, she tugged the page from the typewriter and read it aloud.

What a change a week can bring! Since I last wrote all turned rotten—literally— in the playland of Grand Lake.

Nana stopped to smile at Maggie and Alma, enjoying her own cleverness.

This has not been the scenic land of our vacation dreams, but a smelly site of backed-up sewers! The water table rose in Grand Lake, and with it wells and leach fields have been compromised!

I discovered the first sign of foulness while trolling on the lake. As I watched the lazy progress of my fishing lure on the water, what should pass me but a head of lettuce, bobbing along in the current!

Further investigation by your guest columnist has established two culprits. First, the village of Grand Lake blatantly releases its sewage into the Colorado River. In the past, downstream of the lake was just farmland, with no one to care. Now that the river is subsumed by a reservoir at the dumping spot, and the water from the reservoir is pumped into Grand Lake, the offal is coming right back at us!

"Subsumed?" Maggie asked. "What is that? Why not just say 'covered'?"

"Because 'subsumed' is a 49¢ word and 'covered' is about 19¢." Nana looked at Maggie over her reading glasses, expecting her to get it, which of course Maggie did, although she wouldn't choose to spend her money that way.

No Kansas town, no matter how small, would conscience such a cavalier system.

"'Cavalier'?" asked Maggie, laughing. "Sounds more like a knight on a white horse than an 'offal system'."

"No, I think it's a good choice," Alma said.

"You do?" Nana removed her reading glasses and scrutinized Alma.

"'Cavalier' can mean 'arrogant', which works just fine," Alma said, bending over to dust a lower bookshelf.

Nana resumed her reading:

The second culprit is the federal government, which oversees Kansans and Coloradoans alike; we are close bedfellows. Its grandiose scheme called the Colorado-Big Thompson Project has succeeded in irrigating croplands around Greeley, Colorado, but has neglected its promise to study and maintain the pristine clarity of the waters of Grand Lake. As the citizens of Greeley and the plains reap a bountiful harvest, algae blooms stretch their furry green tentacles into the now-murky waters of Grand Lake. Add to this the stench of backed-up plumbing!

Take up pen to address your Congressmen, dear readers! We must demand that SC80 be funded and its integrity upheld. The language of this bill mandates that the Colorado-Big Thompson Project be operated 'to preserve the fishing and recreational facilities and the scenic attractions of Grand Lake, the Colorado River, and the Rocky Mountain National Park.' Do not let your fair neighbor state suffer further decay!

"Where'd you get the SC80 stuff?" Maggie asked.

"By thoroughly perusing the stack of papers Frank brought home from the town meeting last night. Your grandfather is an excellent editor and columnist, and I don't mean to criticize. But he does not, as a rule, in my opinion, always consult the wide array of sources available to him," said Nana. Then she continued. . . .

Imagine our distress at expecting Friday's visit from Mr. and Mrs. George Goodwin and their collegiate daughter Helen. Your editor and columnist is fly-fishing on the streams today. Would that we all could be up there, where the air is pure and life is ever tranquil! But we will set the cabin to rights now that the scourge has subsided, and keep the home fires burning, because life must go on, including life's social obligations. And so our government must keep its obligations as well.

Nana probably wanted Maggie to clap or say, "Bravo!" but Maggie concentrated on finding the location of a puzzle piece.

"What do you think, Maggie?" Nana asked. This was terrible. It meant so much to Nana that she had to ask for a compliment, and Maggie could only tell her the truth.

"Maybe you shouldn't ask me, Nana, because I haven't learned that kind of writing in school yet. I've got limited exposure, you know."

"Oh. I see."

"What about you, Alma? Do you have limited exposure too?"

"No, ma'am, but it is a departure from what Mr. Hamilton generally writes, and what he writes makes folks look forward to reading the back page of the paper on a Saturday night."

"Change can be a good thing," Nana reasoned, settling back to the typewriter to check her work for errors. After finding it to her satisfaction, Nana folded the column in thirds to fit into an envelope and addressed the front of it in preparation to make the afternoon mail, while Grandpa was fly-fishing.

In the late afternoon, Maggie returned from the Laun-Dro-Mat with Alma, and helped her stretch the sheets across the clotheslines in the backyard and anchor them in place with clothespins. While Alma put the rest of the laundry out on the lines, Maggie sat on a boulder with her Girl Scout pocketknife and whittled on a piece of wood, coaxing a thunderbird to life, which was a fine idea except for its skinny legs and neck.

When Grandpa got home in the late afternoon, Nana met him on the back porch and reminded him to be prepared to give over his fishing duds to Alma the next morning to wash before he took George Goodwin on the streams with him on Saturday.

Grandpa replied, "Goodwin's a talker, Janie, and you know how I feel about that. I'd as soon dunk Goodwin as fish with him, and if he doesn't like the smell of me, he can shop with you ladies until sundown. Don't go there with me, Janie, not with these meetings gobbling up my fishing time."

Nana entered the house without a comment, and Grandpa unloaded his fishing things on the porch and reached into the icebox for a Coca Cola.

Then Uncle Max came 'round the house. He opened a creaky door that looked like a closet on the back of the cabin, but really lead to a darkroom. He went in, came out, and walked down to the maid's cabin door. Maggie repositioned herself on the rock so that she could watch what came next.

Alma pulled apart the Venetian blind on her door to see who was there, then cracked open the door. "Mr. Max, I'm off duty this evening. What is it you want?" In fact, Alma had trotted down the hill to her cabin, with her big hips swaying, jolly as she passed Maggie on the rock because she said, "The day's work's done, and the party's begun."

"Will you help me for just a few minutes? I need to get my darkroom set up. I hadn't planned on it being such a mess." Max's face was salmon-colored with sunburn, except for rings of white around his eyes from his sunglasses.

"Ordinarily I wouldn't mind, but I have a social engagement this evening," Alma replied. Maggie could tell by her stretch of arm holding open the door that Alma already had on her bathrobe.

"You do?"

"Yes, I do!"

"Well, it doesn't need to take us long. Can you help me out here, please?" Max put his hands on his hips and glared at Alma.

Alma pursed her lips and looked at him evenly. She lifted her left arm and pulled up her robe sleeve dramatically to expose her man's Timex watch, and studied it. "If we can do it in eighteen minutes," she said. "That's what I can spare."

Max folded his arms across his chest and looked sideways, away

126

from her. "Come on, Alma, I'm not supposed to be doing the cleaning around here."

"And isn't that a goooood thing?" said Alma. "But there is a time for every purpose. A time to fix breakfast and a time to wait 'til dinner. A time to clean up the house, and a time to play cards with your friends."

"Come on, Alma," Max sighed. "Let's quit using up our eighteen minutes."

"All right." Alma slammed her door, then reappeared in her chartreuse uniform. She jiggled up the incline to the back of the cabin, so that Maggie suspected she had not latched herself back into her underwear. Then she stooped to enter the small door made out of the same bark-slab siding as the rest of the house, so that you hardly noticed it was there unless you were looking for it. When she came back out she headed for the back porch, muttering.

"Like entering the underworld . . . a trashy underworld."

She returned with a pail that reeked of ammonia, two rags, a broom, a dustpan, and a trashcan. She stuck out the broom handle toward Max at the entrance. "I'll take over the counter. You sweep the floor."

But it's a dirt floor. How do you sweep a dirt floor?"

Alma took the broom, swept at the ground with short, vigorous strokes, then gave it back to Max.

Maggie couldn't resist peeking inside. Alma's strong arms scrubbed the counter and the sink quickly and efficiently—rubbing the counter, rinsing and wringing the rag in the pail, rubbing and rinsing again. When she finished with the counters, she wiped down the walls, and then tended the counter running along the back wall of the room. Uncle Max fumbled to handle the broom and hold the dustpan at the same time, but managed to get his sweepings into the trashcan. Then Alma looked at her Timex, gathered up the cleaning supplies, and jiggled away.

"Want to help me set up the equipment, Maggs?" Uncle Max asked her with a grin.

"Sorry," Maggie said, and fled.

About an hour later, while Nana was cooking dinner, Maggie saw Alma and Francine, the maid from next door, walking to the road, each carrying casserole dishes wrapped in tea towels to keep them hot. Francine wore a green and blue print shirtwaist dress and high heels, and Alma wore a navy blue pleated skirt, a blue-and-white checked blouse, and her black cowboy boots. Both women wore red lipstick and earrings of considerable caliber, and they climbed into the backseat of the Mickelson's two-tone green Buick Century Sedan, which was driven by the Mickelson's chauffeur and cook, Jackson. Maggie could feel the car jiggle with laughter as they drove away.

Happy as she was for Alma, a pang of homesickness struck Maggie that sent her to her bedroom to take solace in the successful, dangerous dealings of her friend Nancy Drew, who never seemed to get homesick. Or be thwarted by a grandmother or fickle friends. And as for a Ned Nickerson—it was, of course, Uncle Max who would soon find romance, and he so didn't deserve it.

Mix and Match

ON THE MORNING that the Goodwins were expected, Maggie came downstairs to find a bowl of Corn Flakes and orange juice set out for her, and a parade out back. Still in his pajamas and slippers, Uncle Max had snatched up his clothes into his arms and was walking to the bedroom on the side of the maid's cabin, trailing socks and boxer shorts in his wake, which Alma picked up for him, following along.

After she got Max situated, Alma cleaned up the scant breakfast dishes, changed Max's bed linens, and then commandeered Maggie to help her prepare the requisite Fresh Coconut Cake. Maggie's job was to sit on the red kitchen stool and read aloud to Alma the instructions for high altitude baking from *The Joy of Cooking*.

"Cake doughs at high altitudes are subject to a pixie-like variation that often defies general rules. Read the comments and then launch forth on your own, keeping records at first until you know what gives the greatest success," read Maggie.

"'Pixie-like?'" Alma scrunched up her cheeks.

"At 7,000 feet," Maggie continued—

"What're we at?"

"8,367 feet," said Maggie.

"Go on, then."

"—decrease double-acting baking powder by ¼ teaspoon for every teaspoon called for. Decrease sugar by 2 to 3 tablespoons for each cup indicated and increase liquid by 3 to 4 tablespoons for each cup in the recipe. Raise the baking temperature about 25 degrees."

"Do you really have to do this, Alma?" asked Maggie.

"To the letter, Baby Girl."

Alma poured the batter evenly between the three pans, and when the thermometer on the oven rack registered 225 degrees, she staggered the pans in the oven so that air could circulate around them, and closed the oven door. Then Alma looked heavenward, her smooth lips moving in beseechment of God's seal of approval on her Fresh Coconut Cake.

"Do you ever get tired of cooking?" Maggie asked as they stood together at the sink, washing and drying the bowls and utensils.

"Sometimes I get tired of the cooking part. Mostly because my feet are screaming and my back aches. But I never get tired of bringing folks to the table." Alma gave her a smile.

While Alma kept vigil over the cake, they drank Coca Colas and Maggie summarized for her some of her favorite parts in *The Mystery of the Tolling Bell.*

"When Nancy Drew and her chums Bess and George arrive in a vacation town, they hear that there are a mysterious ghost and a tolling bell in the mouth of a cave up the beach. These always warn boaters away from the mouth of the cave just before a deluge of water roars from the cave to capsize their boats and drown them."

"Um hmmmm," said Alma, as she wiped flour off the counters. "How old are these girls that they're going on vacation by theirselves?"

"It never says. I've wondered. They must be in high school, because Ned Nickerson is in college and he's older, but the mysteries always seem to happen during school vacation."

"I see," said Alma.

"The three girls immediately boat to the cave and explore it, climbing onto a ledge."

"Oh, my."

"And get this, Alma. You would have drowned in the lake the other day, if it hadn't been for what I learned from this story. In the book, George has fallen off the ledge into the water and Bess dives in to save her, using the tired swimmer's carry."

"What's the tired swimmer's carry? Is that how you saved me from drowning, because I don't remember you doing that."

"It's when I had you lie on your back and float, and I cupped my hand under your chin and swam a side-stroke and pulled you along."

Alma cocked one eyebrow at Maggie.

"You were thrashing around too much, or I would have done this," Maggie explained. "I wanted to do it. And listen to this—in the story Bess, realizing her cousin no longer could help herself, grasped her in the cross chest carry and pulled her through the water."

"I don't remember any cross chest carry neither," said Alma.

"There is no way I could get my arm across your chest, even to save your life! That's why I had to think quickly and hail the tourist boat and the volunteer firemen. The point is to assess the situation and do whatever is necessary to save people in dire distress," Maggie explained. "That's what Bess did in the story; that's what ND would do, and I would too."

"Well, I can tell you those volunteer firemen need to be more gentle with their hooks and rings." Alma lowered herself onto a kitchen chair as if she was still sore from the ordeal.

"How did you learn how to do all these here carries?" Alma asked.

"Junior Life Saving in Girl Scouts. I paid better attention than the other girls, because I figured some day I would have to use it."

"I'm sorry the holds didn't work better for you, Alma," Maggie said.

Alma enveloped her in a hug which felt warm and pillowy, and from which Maggie first noticed the aroma of Fresh Coconut Cake.

The timer chimed, and Alma pulled open the oven door. The three cake pans in the dark iron cavern looked ready for Goldilocks. In the back pan, the cake had risen too high and overflowed the sides of the pan. The middle layer had risen perfectly around the sides, but gave up and sank in the center. The third pan—Hallelujah—the third pan was just right.

Alma removed the three pans and set them on wire racks to cool. She hummed as Maggie counted out the marshmallows, and Alma put them in the top of the double boiler, with water boiling in the underneath pan. When the marshmallows had melted, Alma beat them into a frosting. Then she returned to the cooled cake layers. She removed the overflowed layer from it's pan, placed it upside down on the cake plate, trimmed off the over-flowed extra from the edges, and frosted it with firm but gentle strokes of a metal spatula. She sprinkled it with coconut, dressing it up nicely. Maggie watched, mesmerized at Alma's artistry.

Alma topped this layer with the sunken one, filled its swimming pool crater with frosting, and sprinkled it with coconut. Then she carefully lowered the perfect layer onto the top and deftly spread on the stiff, glossy frosting. Maggie gave the cake top shakes of grated coconut.

After admiring her work, Alma placed the cake on top of the icebox on the back porch to stay cool, and suggested that Maggie go find a quiet corner and learn some more about *The Mystery of the Tolling Bell* while Alma put her feet up and refreshed herself before cooking dinner.

When the Goodwins arrived, Nana, Grandpa—who had stayed home from fishing and was cranky—and Max took their guests into town to get hamburgers for lunch.

Maggie sat on the porch floor playing Solitaire when Max held open the porch door so that Helen Goodwin could walk under his arm. He sauntered in behind her with his hands stuck in his pockets all nonchalant, but Maggie knew he was gaga because his cheeks were so red.

"Hi-de-ho," Helen greeted Maggie, who looked up to consider her: golden hair swept fancy at her temples and then hanging bouncy to her shoulders. Big brown eyes with long flittery eyelashes. The sleeves of her playsuit were caught up in bows, showing off tiny tanned shoulders.

"Hi-de-ho," Maggie wiggled her fingers at Helen, then listened as Uncle Max gave Helen a house tour like Nana would do.

"The rugs are Navajos," he said.

"They're swell," Helen replied.

"Lots of books. Looks like y'all like to read."

"Yeah. Course the newspaper's are Pop's."

"Who's reading *Seven Keys to Baldpate*?" Helen picked up the book from the end table. "We just stayed at the Baldpate Inn in Estes, and it was the cat's meow. So quaint!"

"Mother is. Pops has a Bureau of Reclamation meeting in Estes next week, and he promised Mother he'd take her to dinner at Baldpate."

"They must take a key."

"A what?"

"It's a marketing gimmick. The novel was so popular that now the innkeeper asks guests to bring or send a key to leave at the Inn. Thousands of them hang from the rafters in their key room, from all over the world, each tagged with where they're from and who sent them."

"Oh," Max said.

"What about you?" Helen asked.

"Beg pardon?"

"What do you read?"

Sheesh, thought Maggie. He sounds as bright as a boulder.

"Magazines and newspapers mostly," Max replied. "I'm fascinated with photography."

Better, Uncle Max.

"What kinds of photographs?"

"I take photos for Pop's paper, but also anything that catches my fancy. I have a darkroom under the house. Would you like to see it?"

As they walked through the kitchen to the back porch door, Maggie could hear Helen's "Ooooow!" over Alma's Fresh Coconut Cake, and a tiny worry brought Maggie creeping into the kitchen, willing herself invisible.

"Is this the cake Daddy raves about?" asked Helen, bending for a closer look.

Max bent too, over her cleavage. "Must be," he said. "Alma's the best cook around. Here, see what you think." He swiped his index finger around the seam where the cake met the plate, then held his finger to her lips. Helen licked off the sticky sweetness. As her tongue retrieved frosting from the corners of her mouth, she smiled at Max, her eyelashes fanning her eyes.

Max swayed and grabbed the edge of the icebox for support as Helen's finger took a swipe at the frosting, and held it out for him. Maggie nearly choked.

"Ahem." Maggie said from the doorway, her arms folded across her chest.

"Uncle Max, you'd better leave our cake alone," she said.

"Come on Maggs, we're only admiring it. No one will even notice."

"Alma will." The cake now had a bare highway running around the bottom.

"So what?" Max asked.

Helen looked out the porch screen into the yard, distancing herself.

"I made it with her, and it matters to me, Uncle Max. Lots."

"Maggie, you make too big a deal of things," Max said, pushing the screen door open and holding it for Helen to walk through, under his arm.

At 6:30 p.m., Alma and Maggie watched from the porch as the sunset cruise completed its course, and Grandpa and Nana brought their guests up to the cabin for dinner. Alma wore her dress-up black uniform and starched, ruffled white apron, lacking only a squash blossom necklace to set it off perfectly. She looked as though her memories of a week of scrubbing muck from sinks and tubs and toilets had vanished in sparkle dust. A white starched cotton tiara crowned her curly head, and Maggie wanted it. It had great costume potential.

Alma had set the dining room table with the cabin's best: a red-and-white checked tablecloth and matching napkins, a Mexican wrought-iron candle holder with seven lighted red candles, and Nana's cobalt blue Fiestaware.

Nana and Grandpa sat at their usual places at the head and foot of the table, while Maggie and Max sat with their backs to the lake, across from the three Goodwins. Maggie tried to do exactly as Alma had told her and watch Nana for clues as to how to be polite. She spread her napkin on her lap, then picked up the smaller fork for the Vegetable Aspic Salad—which was not her favorite, but she had been warned to forget about her food opinions for the night. It was a small price to pay, really, with the Fresh Coconut Cake coming.

"Helen, I'm thrilled that you've pledged Kappa. Our Adele was a Theta at KU, you know, until she quit school to marry Jack," Nana chattered as they forked their jiggling aspics.

"Maggie, you'll be a Theta someday," said Mrs. Goodwin.

"Oh, I don't think so," said Maggie. She looked up from her plate to find the women's faces fastened on her.

"Well, you know," Maggie waved her fork offhandedly, not knowing what else to say. How should she know if she would go to college, or where, or would like the sorority thing, much less the Theta people? Sororities seemed like a deep dose of Nana to her.

"Maggie, dear, you would do well to watch Helen while she's here, to see how a young lady conducts herself. Sororities provide the best training in social skills, as well as being a place to find enduring friendships," Nana said.

Maggie gazed across the table at Helen, who poked at her trout and acted as though the conversation rode above her head.

"Yes, I agree," said Uncle Max, thoughtfully. "I've joined SAE at KU, and I find that the Greeks help a person learn to make the most in life from any social situation."

Maggie hated the stuck-uppity look on Uncle Max's face. This Uncle Max wasn't the fun uncle that she had worshipped when she was a child. She not only didn't worship him now, she didn't respect him much either. But then what about his record, "The Whiffenpoof Song," that she'd scratched and blamed on Alma? Her guilt over this festered, so that she didn't respect herself very much either, and wanted it to be somehow Uncle Max's fault. Maggie pressed the heel of her cowgirl boot into the top of Max's shoe next to her foot under the table—just because.

"Ow! What was that about, Maggie?" Max howled, much louder than he needed to.

"May I please be excused, Nana?" Maggie asked.

"No, dear, you just settle down and eat your dinner. I don't know what's gotten into you." Nana placed her slender, nail-polished fingers over Maggie's hand and applied a hint of pressure.

"Do give us more news from Topeka," Nana chirped, looking at her guests. After that, they talked about upcoming weddings and predictions for Washburn University's football season.

When Alma cleared the dinner dishes, she asked, "Miss Maggie, could you kindly come help me serve dessert?"

"You may be excused, Maggie," Nana said, so Maggie took her plate and followed Alma into the kitchen.

"Miss Maggie, did you embellish my cake?" Alma asked solemnly, her hands on her black taffeta-ed hips.

Maggie explained that the cake had been violated by Max's pokey finger, which was slicked by Helen, whom Max couldn't take his eyes from the front of, and also by Helen's slinky finger, and so Maggie had repaired the damage with white paste and rice kernels.

Alma stood with her mouth open, processing. Then she looked up at the corner of the kitchen ceiling, then down at Maggie, with telltale laughs playing at the corners of her mouth. She hugged Maggie to her bosom, not checking to be sure she had wiped her mouth with her napkin, although Maggie had.

"We'll just serve up this cake from the kitchen, and who will notice a little surgery to remove an inch from this bottom layer?" Alma said.

"Except from Uncle Max's and Helen's pieces," Maggie said. "Those have to be complete, don't you think?"

"'Of course." Alma smiled wide and picked up the knife.

Alma cut the slices, cleanly slipping them onto the dessert plates, and Maggie delivered them to the table.

"Alma, is this the same cake you served us in Topeka?" Mr. Goodwin asked.

"Yes, sir, this is my Fresh Coconut Cake," Alma stood in the doorway, smiling.

"And I helped her," Maggie said to absorb the glow of approval.

"Excellent," he said. "But still, I don't think it quite compares with my mother's Devil's Food Delite. What do you think, Martha?"

"Oh, I quite disagree," said Mrs. Goodwin, and Maggie heard her whisper to Nana that she'd never cared for either her mother-in-law *nor* the woman's Devil's Food Delite.

Max picked at something between his teeth with the tines of his fork, and Maggie did not like the look that connected him to Helen across the table—a naughty, scheming look if she had ever seen one.

17

Back on the Case

THE SUNLIGHT SEEMED clarified and pure after days of dreary rain, and Saturday all day through there wasn't a cloud in the sky except little cotton balls that don't mean any harm. A brisk breeze tossed sparkles on the water.

Mrs. Goodwin and Nana sat in the gazebo in big floppy sun hats, knitting and gabbing. Uncle Max entertained Mr. Goodwin by pitching horseshoes with him, while Helen sunbathed on the sideline. Grandpa went fishing early, before the company was up.

Everyone commented on what a perfect summer day it was in every way, except Maggie. She could not help but notice that Jamie and Bebo had friends over on their beach for the day, and acted as though they didn't see her on her beach, alone. Or maybe they saw her and didn't care, or they saw her and wanted to rub in what fun they were having without inviting her, even though she thought they'd had fun with her during the poopy days house parties at the Wyatt's.

In the afternoon, Nana took her guests for a boat ride in the Adele to watch the sailboat races. With the three adults in the front seat and Uncle Max with his arm around Helen in the backseat, Maggie got to sit on the wooden motor box, which suited her just fine. But as the breeze disappeared and the boat idled alongside the stymied sailboats, Maggie listlessly swayed with the boat, squinting her eyes against the glare on the water. The sun prickled the part in her hair and cooked her inside her orange life jacket.

Later, when they all came inside to rest and get out of the sun, Maggie found that Alma had gotten the mail, which included a letter from her father. Her heart skipped when she recognized his hand-writing on the envelope.

Wednesday, August 20, 1947
Dear Magpie,

I'm so glad that you are there, because it's so hot here, and the bugs are out in force because it's harvest time. Your mother doesn't get out much and is uncomfortable, but the doctor says everything looks fine.

I've been trying to make the dog hunt, as they say, and sold a good policy last week. But the days are longer when you're gone, Magpie. When you get home I'll take you to the fair and win you a Kewpie Doll. (Ha! This was their joke because he knew she disliked Kewpie dolls.)

Love from
Daddy

Maggie felt smothered by adult worries. Her vacation had slowed into baking, reading, and boring being. And she could tell her daddy was unhappy without her. She had to do something or she would go off her rocker before the last week was up. She lay on her bed until time to dress for dinner and let her brain go neutral.

Dinner meant dressing up when Nana and Grandpa had company, and tonight they were going to the Pine Cone Inn for dinner and dancing—Maggie too. Fortunately, dress up in Grand Lake was entirely different than dress up at home, and Maggie was actually excited to wear the squaw skirt of tiered bandana material and rick rack that Nana had bought for her at Thunderbird's. She was even allowed to wear her red cowgirl boots. But not her cowgirl hat. Nana walked by Maggie's bedroom as she was getting ready, knocked, and offered Maggie her silver and turquoise barrette to wear in her hair, if she would be careful with it. How would she hurt it, Maggie wondered, chew on it? Play Tiddlywinks with it? Nana brushed out Maggie's hair and placed the barrette securely and in just the right place.

When it was time to go, they all sat in the living room waiting for Helen. And waiting. And waiting. "Martha, can't you go up and hurry her along?" Mr. Goodwin asked, and Mrs. Goodwin climbed the stairs. Then they all waited for her too.

When Helen finally appeared, Maggie's mouth dropped open. Helen wore a fertility symbol of the Pueblo Indians, although Maggie hoped she didn't know that's what it was. Right there, hovering above her bosoms on the outside of her fringed white western shirt was a big-as-you-please squashed blossom necklace. It didn't look bold like it did on Alma. It overpowered the girl, making her look top heavy over her blue jeans and cowgirl boots. The final straw was that Helen wore a white cowgirl hat, with the little white bead holding the two strings together just under her pretty chinny chin chin. This was not fair. Maggie looked at Nana, who registered only a smile of pleasure at Helen's outfit.

Maggie asked if she could ride to the Pine Cone with Uncle Max and Helen, instead of in the adult car, and Nana said she could. Once in the backseat of Uncle Max's car, she leaned forward between them and asked,

"Helen, where did you get a squashed blossom necklace?"

Helen fiddled with the silver trumpets that fanned out on both sides of the necklace, straightening them. "Wouldn't you like to know? Max tells me you are quite the amateur detective, so perhaps you can tell me, hmmm? And besides, it's *squash* blossom."

Uncle Max smiled but looked straight ahead.

Why was Helen being ridiculous? It got Maggie's dander up, so that she decided she would show her and figure it out.

"All right then, will you answer three questions?" Maggie asked.

Uncle Max glanced at Helen, his eyebrows up.

"Sure," said Helen, as she looked into the little round mirror in her compact and re-applied her minutes-old lipstick. "But the answers have to be "yes" or "no."

"Okay. Did you get it in Colorado?"

"Yes."

"Did you get it this summer?"

"Yes."

"Did you buy it?"

"No."

Maggie studied Max's face in the semi-darkness of the car. This was crazy. Of course it would be impossible for Helen to have Mrs. Haggerty's necklace. Wouldn't it? In a way, Maggie didn't even care whether she did or not. She was excited for a resurfacing of squashed blossom necklace intrigue. In fact, here was a brand new sub-mystery. How did Helen get her squashed blossom necklace?

Maggie had one more question, but she would save it for Mrs. Goodwin, who didn't know the three questions rule.

The Pine Cone Inn was the hottest nightspot in a very small town. Everybody was at the Pine Cone on a Saturday night, from cowboys in jeans and boots to city slickers in suits. The women wore full skirts, western blouses and Indian silver belts, or their city dancing dresses and high heels. Maggie sat at a long log table with their party and watched the kaleidoscope whirl of Jitterbug and fox trotters to Wayne Karr and his 10 piece orchestra direct from Chicago, as the sign announced at the foot of the bandstand. But the band wore western wear and looked to Maggie like they hadn't seen Chicago for a long time.

The Pine Cone Inn looked like a room soaked in honey: pine paneled walls, pine log tables and benches, and pinecone lamp shades on the chandeliers. A huge round fireplace dominated the center of the room, empty of flame on a warm August night.

The adults ordered cocktails, and then dinner, and about the time Maggie was weary of watching the dancers and of sizing up what they had on, and who danced the best and who danced the worst, she had slipped down so much that her cheek was propped on her hand. Suddenly Grandpa stood by her side, offered her his hand, and asked her to dance.

Grandpa didn't dance like anybody else, more old fashionedy, like a woman who keeps styling her hair in a way that looked gorgeous on her a long time ago, but doesn't any more. He told her his dance had a name—the Collegiate Strut. He probably thought it was hip because of the word "college" in it. He put his right arm around Maggie's waist, and she put her left arm on his back, and they strutted around the floor to the music.

Maggie loved it; so easy and fun, with her grandpa animated and his chest stuck out. They took their laps around the periphery of the dance floor, then through the center and out again, staying out of the paths of the rowdier dancers, but gaining good mileage and a great dance-floor view.

As the evening advanced, Grandpa strutted with Nana, and he strutted with Mrs. Goodwin, but he seemed happiest when he strutted with Maggie. That is, until Helen cut in and invited Grandpa to strut with her. The way Grandpa beamed at Helen and held her around her little waist embarrassed Maggie. The collegiate Strut now looked fuddy-duddy, and Maggie didn't want to do it any more.

Max had been sitting on the pine bench at their table between Maggie and Helen. When Maggie returned to the bench, he was jiggling his leg constantly, even though Maggie clamped her hand on his knee now and then to force a temporary pause. Meanwhile, Helen danced with most of the men in the room, all ages of them, while Max sat and jiggled his leg.

Finally Max danced the Jitterbug with Helen, but he looked stiff and jerked Helen around like a stuffed doll. Helen was no rag doll.

Maggie grew bored and decided to make a trip to the restroom. On her route, she spied Mrs. Haggerty sitting with another old lady, looking bereft of her jewels. She seemed shriveled and harmless, and she had tried to make up to Nana on the telephone, so Maggie sat down on the pine bench across from her.

"Hello, Mrs. Haggerty."

"Hello, dear. Now who are you?"

"I'm Maggie, Mrs. Hamilton's granddaughter. Remember . . . the squashed blossom necklace?"

"Oh, yes. It's *squash* blossom, dear." Mrs. Haggerty raised her chin to gain elevation. She sat slightly tilted over, and Maggie didn't think she had the strength to support the weight of a *squash* blossom necklace anyway, but there you were.

"Maggie," Mrs. Haggerty leaned forward and grasped Maggie's warm hands in her cold, bony ones. "You can give up worrying about my necklace. I'm sure my daughter-in-law from Louisiana has taken it. She has stolen things from me in the past: jewelry, money, even my drain board in the kitchen."

Maggie cocked her head. Drain board?

"Has she been here to visit you recently?" Maggie wished she had a little pad with her on which to take notes, and her fringed leather jacket.

"No, the last time I saw her was six months ago, and if I never see her again, that will be too soon." Mrs. Haggerty's eyes hardened and she drew her hands away.

"That's interesting, Mrs. Haggerty, because I had a new bit of evidence, and I wondered if you might have given it to a girl named Helen. She's here; let me see if I can find her. There. On the dance floor, to the far right with my Uncle Max. Do you see her necklace?"

Mrs. Haggerty squinted so hard that Maggie couldn't imagine

she could see Helen, much less Helen's necklace.

"Yes. Yes. That does look like mine. But I don't know her, so how could I have given it to her? Maybe she stole it from me. You send her over here to talk to me. Go on. Go get her." She shooed Maggie off with her long bony hands.

But Maggie, thinking better of this, said that she had been on her way to the restroom and had to go real bad, and fled to hide in a stall and think. Helen had just arrived in town, and why would a certified Kappa Kappa Gamma steal an old lady's *squash* blossom necklace? She should have thought of that before she brought it up.

As she snuck from the restroom toward the dance floor, Maggie heard Mrs. Haggerty calling after her, "Have her come over here, now."

Maggie turned around to wave at Mrs. Haggerty, and made a bee-line for Mrs. Goodwin, but discovered she had left their table. Nana, Grandpa, and Mr. Goodwin were gone too.

"Come on, Maggie," Uncle Max said. "I'm supposed to take you home."

"But don't you and Helen want to stay?"

"Nope, I've got other plans. Clear night. Full moon." Uncle Max winked at Maggie.

Maggie glanced back at Mrs. Haggerty, who was still watching her, and practically pushed Helen and Uncle Max out of the Pine Cone Inn.

Back in the kitchen at Kawuneeche, Alma wiped the last dinner plate and oiled the cast iron skillet, and she placed a glass dome over the surviving slices of her Fresh Coconut Cake. Brushing the last rice grains from the cake plate, she chuckled. That Maggie was loyal, she'd give her that. In fact, Alma wondered if deep down she'd come with the Hamiltons because Maggie filled a hollow place. It'd been easier not to have children, with Baxter's traveling, and her working six days a week. But would easier hold their future together? For that matter, did the *easier* of their lives conveniently keep them apart? Funny how when you got away to a far different place, you started to sort things out.

Alma was very young when Baxter began to frequent her mother's restaurant. She hadn't had a chance to decide whether she really loved him, or maybe would better love someone else. There was always Baxter. So it caught her by surprise to miss him now, and worry about him a little.

As Alma walked to her cabin, the evening was unusually balmy, and stars canopied the sky, begging her to not give in and go to bed just yet. Alma removed her starched white cotton tiara and ruffled apron and hung up her best black uniform. She peeled off her shoes and released her captive bunions. Then she slipped on a skirt and blouse, a sweater, and her red moccasins, and, guided by her flashlight beam, picked her way between the rocks and trees down the steps to the lake.

To her surprise, she resisted the old pattern that would take her safely along the path to the gazebo, and walked toward the swing on the end of the dock. Usually she would see it hanging dark and forebodingly close to the deep water. But tonight it was suspended under the stars, a chariot swung low for her.

Alma took slow, careful footsteps, keeping her eyes fixed on the swing ahead rather than the water gently lapping the docksides. Next she gingerly lowered herself onto the swing. Its puny chains and slats were a definite concern, but they held her, in a sparkling land where she had never been before.

As the moon rose from over a peak, it rolled out a carpet of sparkles on the lake that ended not far from her feet. She felt like she could step onto it, the light bearing her up above the dark deep. "Lord," she whispered, "are those sparkles for me?" The glittering path across the lake, and the panoply of celestial lights above it gave Alma courage, and she began to gently rock in the swing. Tucked into beauty, as her heart filled, her thoughts turned hopeful. She didn't need to fret about Maggie, or Mz Hamilton. Never had she felt such an expansive sense of "beyond." She had conquered a wood stove; she, who had never swum, had survived a humiliating plunge into an icy lake; she had some new friends, and a pair of red moccasins and of black cowboy boots. She willed herself to not even worry about Baxter.

Time passed. The breeze grew cool, but Alma didn't budge.

The adults had gone to bed by the time Max, Helen, and Maggie returned from the Pine Cone Inn. While Helen went upstairs to change before their moonlight boat ride, and Max went to his room out back, Maggie grabbed her fringed leather jacket from the peg by the front porch door and ran down the steps to the lake.

She stopped short of the dock and gasped. A bulky black shadow occupied the swing at the end of the dock. A bear! Maggie recoiled and stood still to consider whether to turn around and tiptoe away or stay. But the figure's head turned to reveal Alma's profile. Tempted as Maggie was to go sit by Alma's side in the moonlight, she had another purpose tonight. So she waited until Alma settled again and crept into the boathouse.

Maggie snuggled down under two beach towels and a couple of life jackets that had been left on the back seat of the Chris Craft, arranging the pile so that no strand of her hair, no flash of red cowgirl boot showed from under it. She experimented with positions, finding how she could be comfortable but also have a view of the front seat over the motor box.

Why was she doing this? For so many reasons that it just felt right. First of all, Uncle Max wasn't about to include her in such fun as a moonlight boat ride, so why shouldn't she arrange it on her own? Then there was her desire to moderate this quick romance. If they needed a chaperone on the boat, Maggie was prepared for the job.

Whatever that meant. If that meant she would gum up the works, it was fine with her. Maggie didn't like either of them very much at that moment.

"Ho there, Alma. Not used to finding you on the dock in the moonlight," Uncle Max called as he and Helen got to the dock. "Don't have a man with you, do ya?"

"Shore wish I did have my man," Alma said. "You two have some fun."

Maggie felt the boat dip to one side as Uncle Max helped Helen into the boat and then climbed into the driver's seat. After the initial starting roar, he idled the boat quietly, so Nana and Grandpa wouldn't rise up in bed, reading into their little adventure.

But once Uncle Max backed the boat out of the boathouse and turned her around, and cruised partway up the lake, he opened it full throttle and Maggie peered from her hiding place. Uncle Max had his arm around Helen's back and she had scooted up tight against him. Glancing backwards, Maggie saw diamonds dancing on the water in the boat's wake.

Helen pulled her cardigan tightly around her shoulders, and her golden hair whipped behind her. She laughed and coaxed Uncle Max to go faster. Maggie huddled down, loving the speed until the boat circled back over its own wake, jumping and slamming against the water, and slamming Maggie against the backseat. Now her neck ached and her right leg was cramping.

Mid-lake, Uncle Max slowed the boat to an idle, and Maggie peeked from her towel nest to see why, and to change her position. Helen's head rested on Uncle Max's shoulder, as he pointed out the Lady of the Lake mountain formation, just as Grandpa had shown Maggie and had probably shown Nana, and long before them an Indian warrior had shown his Indian maiden.

"Can you see her?" Uncle Max asked Helen. "She's lying on her back. Her hair goes off this way. Then comes her profile. Then Baldy is her b—."

Maggie put her hands over her ears and sank under the towels.

When she recovered and surfaced, she figured Helen must have been impressed, because Uncle Max was kissing her. Just a little one. But when Helen seemed to like it, Uncle Max went for it, moving his mouth around on hers, repositioning and kissing again. And again.

Maggie had wondered just how this was done, having been no closer to a schmaltzy kiss than movies staring Clark Gable and Lana Turner. So, holding one of the beach towels over her as camouflage, Maggie slithered slowly across the wooden motor box closer . . . closer . . . closer.

Coming up for air, Helen rolled her head on the back of her seat and looked up at the stars: thousands and millions and billions of them. Then she glanced back at the glittering wake behind the boat. She locked eyes with Maggie and screamed.

Dear Diary, Saturday, August 23, 1947

I hope that Mrs. Goodwin isn't in Nana's bridge club in Topeka, or else I've ruined that bridge club too. That is, if the adults find out about the boat ride tonight. Maybe they won't, because there was the chaperone angle, which I managed pretty well, if you think about it.

I'm not sorry that I did it, except for the part that it scared Alma so badly when Helen screamed that she got up from the swing too fast and nearly fell into the lake. I don't want saving Alma on my conscience again. I'm confused, because when I try to do good things, other people think they're bad things.

I have even more respect for ND. Not only does she solve her mysteries, she does it so that Hannah Gruen and her father Carson Drew and her chums Bess and George and her boyfriend Ned Nickerson all believe she's the champ. Maybe I'm in the wrong line of work.

Sincerely,

Maggie

18

Changes in the Wind

THE GOODWINS STIRRED around too long getting ready to leave. Even Maggie knew you should get an early start to put two or three hundred miles under your tires before the sun seared the Kansas highways in heat mirages. But it took them till 10:20 a.m. to get into the car, while Grandpa paced because he wanted to go fishing.

Helen and Max stood on the dock talking until the last, last minute before the girl had to leave. This made Grandpa furious, since he and Mr. Goodwin had to carry all the luggage.

While Mrs. Goodwin watched the men load the suitcases and tuck-ins into the car, Maggie saw her chance.

"Mrs. Goodwin, may I ask you a question?"

"Of course, dear."

"Do you know where Helen got her *squash* blossom necklace?"

"Well, of course I do, Maggie, because it's *my* squash blossom necklace. Mr. Goodwin bought it for me at Miller's Indian Village in Estes, and it's a particularly fine one, if I do say so."

"So you let Helen wear it last night?"

"She said that when she told Max that I'd purchased one in Estes, he suggested Helen wear it to the Pine Cone Inn. Now that I think of it, he said you'd get a kick out of it. Ha ha ha," Mrs. Goodwin laughed good-naturedly, as if she'd done Maggie a favor.

Ha ha ha, thought Maggie.

After everybody said their good-byes, standing by the Goodwin's car with their arms folded, and then with hugs and handshakes, Maggie sat on a rock in the backyard beneath the clotheslines, playing with the clothespins. She snapped them one to another to make a train. But really she was missing Alma, who was in her cabin this morning, since Sunday was her day off.

Pretty soon Uncle Max entered the little bedroom on the side of the maid's cabin and reappeared carrying his clothes in a jumble. He walked past Maggie with merely a grunt when she said hello, dropping a pair of boxer shorts as he passed her. A worn pair, she just knew it.

At first Maggie ignored them, the blue and red plaid polluting the pine needles. But as Uncle Max climbed the back steps to the cabin, she pinched them in the jaws of a clothespin and waved them around. Max came back down the steps, grabbed them, and flipped off the clothespin.

"Grow up, Maggie," he said, without so much as a glance at her.

In the afternoon, Grandpa was on the stream, Max napped in his real bed, and Alma offered to take Maggie to town for an ice cream soda—leaving Nana in the house alone. She brought her iced tea to the screened-in porch, and sat on the swing to cast off and finish the baby blanket, in good time, since they would leave for home at the end of the week. Adele was due in less than three months, and Janie was allowing herself to believe there would be a healthy new baby in the family before the holidays.

As she knitted, an east wind swept down the mountainside to torment the lake. Within minutes the bossy winds thrashed ridges of waves into frothy white caps.

150

Instinctively, Jane put her knitting aside and stood with binoculars to see if any craft needed help on the lake. A sailboat, one of the flat-bottomed racing scows, tacked toward safe harbor, the crew of four hiked out, bent out backwards on the high side of the boat to keep it aright. Goosebumps rose on Jane's arms as she remembered long-past summers, on a lake in Wisconsin, where her family vacationed, when she was pretty darn good crew. She never let on, to whatever boyfriend was skipper, how the out-of-control flapping of canvas, that sound like firmly flicking a clean sheet over a bed, made her nearly wet her pants. Ah, but the screaming speed, the freedom, the fun!

As the sailboat docked and lowered its sail, and all craft seemed at home, Jane sank into the porch daybed and wrapped herself in a throw blanket, pulling her stockinged feet up under her. She felt small but safe in a pocket as she watched the elements cavort and collide on the lake.

A sea gull taunted the storm. Instead of waiting it out, bobbing on the water or on a limb on the shore, it swooped low and pressed against the wind, suspended immobile two feet above the waves. It turned, circled, then pressed again, as if to prove itself. Or was it for the joy of it?

As the wind moved on to toss boughs in the forest, sheets of rain swept across the lake, heavy at first, each drop punching a hole in the water. Then its vengeance was spent, and soft rain came like a salve. Jane sat damp, her hair plastered to the sides of her face, possessed by the fragrance of rain on the water, rain on the earth, rain on the porch. She was young again, with no responsibilities to schedule, plan, or entertain; no need to move people in the direction their lives ought to go. She was as free as the rain and the wind.

Jane feared she had become her own mother, a woman who watched and worried while her family tried to have fun. She used to chaff against her.

"Oh, don't worry, Mother."

"Why can't you just let us be?"

"We're just having fun."

As a newspaper editor's wife, Jane felt her family lived in a fishbowl. They swam in paper and ink. A family misstep, any scandal or public embarrassment, would appear in print—a competitor's print, a malcontent's print—quicker than the gusts that now scoured the lake.

Shivering on the porch daybed, in the rain, Jane felt cleansed from her many careful years. She was absolved from self-imposed service as God's hovering cloud—go this way, stay here. It was time for Jane Hamilton to find her purpose and to enjoy life, not stifle it. God could very well watch over her and everyone else's adventures.

Jane thought of Maggie, and pictured her strong granddaughter hiking out on a sailboat as it sliced the water and the wind. Why was she continually annoyed with Maggie? For being a child instead of a debutante? Was it something else? Was she jealous of the child? For having a purpose, when Jane still couldn't find her own?

Jane resisted the impulse to go in and dry off, to change clothes and attend to her soaking hair. She sat on the swing, hugging her knees, and let the breeze dry her as she was.

19

Ahoy to Haggerty's

Nana called Mrs. Gerrard on Monday morning, without even asking Maggie, to invite Jamie and Bebo over for lunch and to play. Maggie could hardly believe her good luck. This fit perfectly into her plan. In fact, she decided it was meant to be. Finally.

After lunch, Nana left on a hike to the stream where Grandpa and the Professor were fly-fishing. Alma flopped onto the porch daybed and soon snored softly.

At the card table, Maggie, Jamie, and Bebo played War. Maggie was winning, and her chums were whining. She decided that it was time.

"Today we're going to go to Mrs. Haggerty's cabin to find clues as to the whereabouts of that necklace, as soon as Alma wakes up. Did her daughter-in-law really steal it from her, with the drain board, or did she lose it, or did she hide it somewhere in the house, even from herself? I go home in five days, and I am exactly no where," said Maggie. "I figure I've gotten in so much trouble that I have nothing to lose. I can't go home without solving a mystery, not as boring as my life will be when I get there."

"Just how are you going to get to Haggerty's, Miss Detective?"

Jamie asked. If there was any way to lop off these two from being her chums, Maggie would do it. But Haggerty's was a big cabin, and she would need help. How ND found chums who so thoroughly adored her was beyond Maggie.

"You'll see. But I'll need your help once we get there," said Maggie, watching Alma's chest rise and fall under an opened *Ladies Home Journal*.

"No way," said Jamie. "I sense one of your bad influences coming on."

"Now listen," Maggie said. "I'll split the reward with you."

"Re-ward?" Jamie said. "Do you really think that cranky old lady is going to give you a reward? Don't you understand that she doesn't even care about her necklace?"

But Maggie cared. Mrs. Haggerty probably cared. Why couldn't this mystery be clean like Nancy Drew's? You discover the bad guys. You confront them, with the police or Carson Drew or Ned Nickerson close by. Widows and orphans are saved from destruction. There's a reward to give away. Mrs. Haggerty was even a widow! Maggie didn't get it. But she knew she had to finish it.

"There should be a reward. Do you want it or not?" Maggie asked. "Besides, have you got anything better to do? You want to go home and paint?" Now Maggie was mad at Jamie and her stinking attitude. Look at the fun Maggie had given her this summer.

"Fifty-fifty?" Bebo asked.

"Yep. Fifty for me and fifty for you guys."

Alma snorted twice and rolled over onto her side, so that the *Ladies Home Journal* fell to the floor, startling her. Maggie knew that Alma would not be snoozing on the porch daybed with three children in the house if Nana wasn't off hiking. She figured that Alma would wake up wondering what Maggie had been doing, so Maggie would be vague enough about her behavior to make Alma feel guilty, and then use this guilt to her advantage. Maggie had a plan.

"Alma, can I get you some pop?" Maggie asked as Alma sat up, rubbed the sleep from her face, and peered out at the lake to get a read on the time and the weather.

Alma stared at Maggie, surprised. "Well sure, I'll have a strawberry soda. Thank you."

Maggie fetched a bottle cold from the icebox and flipped off the cap with the bottle opener on the kitchen door jam. Alma took three slugs of soda, facing side-ways to Maggie, her near eye focused large on her, specifically on Maggie's gold leather fringed jacket, which she had put on while fetching the soda. Maggie didn't wait for her question.

"Alma, there's something very important we need help with, and you're the only one who can do it," Maggie said, standing in front of her.

Alma studied the red depths of her soda, looked around the porch, and back at Maggie, and at the jacket fringe. Jamie and Bebo stood up and waited behind Maggie.

"What is it?" Alma burped.

"We've got to find clues at Mrs. Haggerty's cabin. It's our last chance, and since Nana won't take us there, you've got to do it."

Bebo whistled between his teeth. Jamie grabbed Bebo's arm and pulled him toward the porch door. "I think it's time for us to go home," Jamie said.

Bebo wrestled free from his sister's grasp. "Wait!" he said, watching to see what would happen.

"Maggie, you've got no business nosing into Mrs. Haggerty's affairs," said Alma. "Besides, your Grandpa's gone with the car. How am I s'posed to get you there?"

"The outboard. It would be much faster anyway," Maggie replied.

Alma cocked an eyebrow. "Don't you even think about it, Maggie. No more boat rides for me. Period. Ever." Alma moved her hands in a "You're out."

"But we can't go without you."

"Correct."

"What if something happens to us on the lake without you?" Maggie asked.

"But there is no without me. You're not allowed to drive that boat without an adult. Your grandpa's orders."

"Which is why you'd best come so we don't both get in trouble."

Alma rocked back and forth a couple of times to gain momentum, and got up off the daybed. Putting her hands on her hips, she rose up to full glory.

"Maggie, that boat is staying right where it is. You are the stubbornest child! There's something wrong in your head."

"The only thing wrong with my head is you standing there in my way. My first real mystery, and I can't get to it because a big scaredy cat is afraid of the water."

Maggie turned and pushed past her friends through the screened door, shoving it wide for maximum slap shut behind her. She resisted the urge to see if Alma followed her, but she soon heard her puffing for breath as she charged down the steps. Jamie and Bebo scampered after Alma.

At the dock, Maggie motioned for Jamie and Bebo to sit on the front bench seat of the outboard, and glowered at them good so they wouldn't ask questions. Maggie wrenched the painter from the metal ring on the dock, crouched low to board the boat properly, as ND would do, and ripped one full-strength but futile tug on the starter cord of the outboard motor. A second dramatic pull dared the motor to life.

She shoved the throttle into forward, but the boat moved barely inches before it careened to one side. Alma had planted one formidable foot, in a red beaded moccasin, on the middle bench seat, throwing the boat off balance. She hung onto a post on the dock, her sturdy legs forming an upside down V that widened as the boat tipped precariously away from her.

Jamie and Bebo grabbed at metal rings on the dock and pulled the boat back alongside it, closing Alma's V, as Alma whimpered with her eyes closed. Feeling sorry for Alma had not been part of Maggie's plan.

"It's all right, Alma," Maggie assured her, patting her knee. But Maggie still idled the motor so Alma would know this boat was leavin'.

"Now crouch down and grab hold of both gunwales," Maggie instructed.

"What's a gunwale? Don't you play with me, Miss Maggie!"

Maggie jumped out of the idling boat, as the kids held it tight against the dock, to demonstrate her ND crouch again. "Gunwales are the ridges along the top sides of the boat. See? Hold onto them while you get in. That's it. That's it."

Crouching took Alma a few tries. Jamie and Bebo looked away from each other to control their giggles as Alma's substantial rump, in its Monday powder blue uniform, lowered itself to the middle seat in the small craft.

Maggie slipped into the back of the boat by the motor, shifted the throttle into reverse, and they were off, with Alma continuing to grasp the gunwales.

Jamie reached into the space between the front bench seat and the bow to gather life jackets. She handed a puffy orange vest to Bebo, then tied on her own. She tossed one back to Maggie, who flicked it onto the floor of the boat with her free hand.

"Put it on, Maggie. We have to wear them and so do you," said Jamie.

Yes, of course ND would do that. She wouldn't need it, but she would wear it. Maggie let the boat veer toward shore while she used two hands to tie a bowline, a knot known to be secure but easy to undo, in the ties on the front of her life vest.

Jamie handed the last life vest to Alma, who just looked at it in her lap until Jamie and Bebo coaxed her to let go of one gunwale so that she could plunge an arm through one armhole. They tugged it up on her arm until it wedged on her bicep, one side of the vest hugging her back and the other hugging her bosom.

With her crew safely settled, Maggie changed course, from along-the-shoreline to across-the-middle-of-the-lake. Alma, locked in position on the center seat, swiveled her head to scowl at Maggie. Then she faced forward without a word.

"Where are we going?" Bebo asked.

Maggie didn't answer. She drew her pinched thumb and pointy finger across her lips to zip them, to enforce a corporate lip-zipping, and maintained her direct, full-speed route across the lake toward the Haggerty cabin.

"Alma, don't you want to look over the side and try to see the bottom?" Bebo joked, as he leaned over to run his fingers along the water.

"Nope. That bottom is not a happy land," Alma replied.

A mid-afternoon wind frolicked on the lake, kicking it choppy so that the bow of the aluminum boat rose and then slapped the surface, rose and slapped. The breeze cut the heat of what was one of the few perfect sunny August days on this vacation. Soon the glare of sunlight on the rippled lake exerted an inescapable spell, so that Jamie, too, reached out to feel the spray as the little boat slapped over the waves.

A cool spray blew into Maggie's face. The young sleuth felt a thrill of excitement as she guided the craft toward her destination, which might hold a solution to the mystery. Maggie whooped with glee to be finally making the crucial visit to Haggerty's.

Bent forward, Alma would not let go of the gunwales. And yet, when Alma peered back at her, Maggie caught a flash of her white teeth.

In Haggerty's cove, the waters smoothed. Sunbathers on the beach waved to them cheerily, and Alma straightened and noticed that her red beaded moccasins rested in six inches of water in the bottom of the boat. Alma complained that they were ruining her new moccasins, and the kids tried to persuade Alma to pick up her feet. Suddenly, with a bump and a thud the motor swallowed its drone and died.

The passengers looked at Maggie. Maggie looked at the motor. She turned the throttle to neutral and pulled the cord, with no pay. A rock, no doubt, had broken the prop.

"Whatcha gonna do, Nancy Drew?" Bebo asked, squinting at her. Maggie noted with pleasure that his tone implied that he thought she might know.

Would they be dashed on that cruel rock over which the waves were dashing with high-sent spray?

They were drifting about twenty yards off shore. Maggie thought it was Alma's fault for distracting her from watching where they were going, but she didn't want to blame Alma, who had been a good sport all things considered, and whom she had sassed, and who after all wore a ridiculous orange lifesaver around her shoulder.

"Don't even mention swimming, Maggie," Alma said under her breath.

"We're too far out," Maggie said, "But we can row."

Jamie and Maggie pulled the two oars from their metal keepers just under the gunwales and mounted them into the oarlocks, giving the handles to Alma, since she sat in the prime rowing position.

"Miss Maggie, I've had just about enough," said Alma. "This isn't the Navy, and you're not the Admiral."

"Well," Maggie asked, businesslike, "how are we going to row, unless you move to the front of the boat or to the back?"

Alma looked around the boat and seemed to decide that the front seat was too small and the back seat, with the motor, was intimidating.

"Bebo, you sit on my lap here, and you can row," said Alma. "Come on up here." She patted her lap. By this time the onlookers on the shore stood wrapped in beach towels, watching them.

Bebo climbed onto her lap, but this put him so high up that it was hard to get the oars into the water at a proper angle. With one oar he'd swipe at the water, missing it entirely; then he'd over-compensate with the other oar and dig it too deeply beneath the surface, causing the boat to turn in circles.

Maggie despaired of imagining what ND would do—certainly not be up on Alma's lap, so she kept ND out of it. Slowly, slip-shod, the boat inched toward Haggerty's beach. When the water grew shallow, the children took off their Keds to wade to shore. Maggie tugged the boat by its painter, and Bebo and Jamie pushed from behind, with Alma in the center, like an African queen.

Battle at Haggerty's

CORALEE WELCOMED THEM at the porch door, and took Alma's moccasins to put on a sunny rock in the yard to dry. She was a slight, bent Negro woman, like a willow, in a white zip-front uniform. Older than Alma, she had an ample sprinkling of freckles across her cheeks and nose, which intrigued Maggie, who didn't know that Negro people had freckles just like red-headed girls, and she made mental note to ask Alma about this.

Coralee settled in a ladder-back chair, and offered Alma the porch daybed, which was padded and warmed with a wool blanket and large black pillows. Jamie and Bebo sat with the Gingerales that Coralee offered to them, but Maggie stood next to the swing with hers. Coralee had closed the door to the house, because Mrs. Haggerty was napping, and they must not disturb her.

Those freckles on Coralee's cheeks folded up together as she grinned at Alma."Why, Alma, didn't know you'd taken to boating. You wanted to come see me so bad that you rowed over?" Coralee lost herself in laughter. As the moments for replying passed and Alma just sat smiling at Coralee, Maggie realized that Alma had no intention of answering, and was leaving it to her.

"Actually, Coralee," said Maggie, "my grandmother asked her to come. Nana has taken up trolling, as you may know, but she wants Alma to learn to row so she can row her boat sometimes when she doesn't want the engine to disturb the fish, and to be helpful with things like taking the fish off the hook." A sideways glance told Maggie that Alma was giving her the serious eye accompanied by pursed lips.

"And I saw the chance to help Alma practice her rowing," Maggie continued, "and also to remind Mrs. Haggerty just one more time before I go home that I would be happy to help her recover her *squash* blossom necklace as I have an uncanny ability to solve mysteries. Just in case her daughter-in-law didn't steal it."

"Yes, Honey, but you don't need to do that. Your grandmother already asked Mrs. Haggerty to encourage your mystery-solving, so if she wanted to, she would have."

"But Nana told me to let the whole thing be, even though Mrs. Haggerty is without a valuable possession." Maggie was confused, and chewed a fingernail.

"No, Mrs. Haggerty told me that your grandmother asked her to play along in the whole business because you needed something to do," said Coralee.

Something to do? Like Maggie was a child in nursery school! This was perhaps Nana's worst blow.

"Mrs. Haggerty has certainly not been helping me," said Maggie. "In fact, nobody's been helping me! Is Mrs. Haggerty's necklace really missing, or is maybe the whole thing made up so that Maggie will have something to do?" Maggie slapped her thighs and glared at them all.

"Now that I can't say," replied Coralee, sitting back in her stiff chair.

"What do you mean, 'you can't say'?" Maggie asked. "You don't know, or you can't say?"

"Well, I didn't know, but now I can't say." Coralee looked at

Maggie intently with freckled punctuation. Alma studied her bunions. The other kids didn't make a peep.

Coralee was an accomplice in a cover-up, Maggie could clearly see it. Unless, of course, she had stolen the necklace herself. Maggie bit a different nail, pulling it to the quick.

"Coralee, what is it that you know, but won't say? Are you trying to cover up something for Mrs. Haggerty? Or are you trying to cover up something for yourself? You would be the person most likely to have access to the necklace. Do you have it, Coralee?"

Coralee rose indignantly and shoed at the children as if chasing cats out the door. "You children go along back home now. You got no business talkin' to me that a way when I'm just tryin' to do my job."

Alma rose too, and put a big hand gently on Coralee's arm. "Miss Maggie," Alma said, "you owe Carolee an apology. No way has she taken that lady's necklace, and you have no right to accuse her!"

"Okay, I'm sorry, Coralee." Maggie was agonizing because she was digging herself into a hole. "I'm just trying so hard to get to the bottom of this."

"How 'bout you and me go talk in the kitchen," Alma gently steered Coralee by the elbow toward the door to the house.

"Well, all right."

Following Alma, Coralee turned at the door and looked at the children. "But don't you do any rummaging, you hear?" she said, frowning.

"I assure you, Coralee, that we don't rummage," said Maggie.

"The other reason we came, Coralee," Alma said as they walked through the living room, "is that I hear Mrs. Haggerty has a wood stove, and this being something I am just growing accustomed to, I thought you might share with me some of your secrets for cooking on it, you being one of the finest cooks on the lake." Alma reached back and closed the kitchen door behind them.

"What are we doing?" Jamie whispered. "Is this a mystery or not, because we are going to be in a lot of trouble before we get out of here today."

"Are you kidding?" Maggie argued. "Now it's a mystery within a mystery within a mystery. I don't care if we get in trouble; I can't leave this undone."

The kids scurried across the living room and slipped behind the coats hanging on wall pegs until the two maids were safely chattering in the kitchen.

Maggie tested each stair to determine where it might creak the least, taking one step in its center, the next on the right or left, and some stairs on tiptoes, but since Jamie and Bebo clamored heedlessly up behind her, it made no difference.

Three bedrooms and a tiny bathroom opened onto the upstairs hallway. All the doors were open, so they paused and listened before slipping past each room. In the bedroom that overlooked the lake, Mrs. Haggerty slept.

The three children stood at the foot of Mrs. Haggerty's bed, waiting to see if waves from her snores rippled into the room like radar to alert her of their presence. She laid on top of the bedspread, which had been turned down enough to expose the pillow. A red Hudson Bay wool blanket covered her twig-like body, except for her feet. Her bedroom slippers, outside the bottom of the blanket, pointed straight up. Mrs. Haggerty's long nose also pointed straight up, and as Maggie leaned close, she could see gray hairs up her nostrils. The hair on the old lady's head was protected from naptime rumpling by two pin curls next to her face on either side. A sudden snort from the old lady, followed by a whistling crescendo, caused the kids to stiffen. Then the rhythm resumed, and Maggie motioned for them to fan out around the room.

Jamie seated herself at the dressing table that had a jewelry box on top. Of course Jamie didn't find a squash blossom necklace, but she did find large, rhinestone-encrusted earrings that she clipped onto her ears. She picked up a silver-handled comb, but upon seeing it had collected gray hairs, she replaced it on the dressing table.

Bebo pulled open the curtain that formed a door to the old lady's clothes closet, and smashed the garments to the center of the closet on their hangers so that he could investigate the hooks on the closet walls that had belts, handbags, slips and nightgowns festooning from them.

Crouching on her hands and knees to look under the bed, Maggie found three suitcases in graduated sizes, each with the initials LGH below the tiny hole for a key. Lying on her stomach and trying each latch, she found them all locked. This was further evidence that the necklace had been stolen. Anyone who locked her suitcases to store them empty under her bed didn't lose track of belongings willy-nilly.

Slowly Maggie tugged at the medium-sized suitcase, unable to resist the opportunity to pick a lock. As she pulled, the suitcase banged against the mattress springs, jolting the bed. Mrs. Haggerty's eyes flew open and met Jamie's eyes in the mirror over the dressing table. Mrs. Haggerty screamed a high, shrill, anemic, old-lady-on-her-back sort of screech.

Jamie tossed the earrings, missing the jewelry box. She upset the dressing table stool as she fled from the room to hide in an adjoining bedroom. Bebo yanked the curtain closed and hid behind the clothes in the closet.

"Help! Help! Help!" Mrs. Haggerty cried baby screams from her bed. She shook her hands in the air as if grabbing for heavenly aid.

Maggie shoved the suitcases further under the bed and laid under there alongside them.

Coralee ran to the bedside and gathered Mrs. Haggerty's hands in her own, lowering them to the blanket. "Shush. Shush. Mrs. Haggerty, it's all right," she crooned.

Soon the strip of light from the room grew dark and anger-filled eyes in a bandana-framed face fixed on Maggie underneath Mrs. Haggerty's bed.

Dear Diary, Monday, August 25, 1947
My entire vacation is now a miserable failure. The worst is,

I have failed to solve a mystery that ND would have wrapped up on about Day 3. Carson Drew would have paid to repair an outboard motor at a snap, but Grandpa says he's tempted to take it out of my allowance. I don't get any allowance up here, so I hope that means he's joking. But he sure looked mad.

Then there's Hannah Gruen. Nancy Drew would have fainted from Alma's glaring at her, inches from her own face, which was squished in generations of dust under an old lady's bed. I did not faint, although I can see now the great convenience of a fainting spell. Of course Nana was so mad that I made Alma take us in the boat that a vein thumped out on her forehead, but I think that I got the bigger fright overall than Alma did.

And ND's trusted friends? Jamie and Bebo's mother won't let them leave their beach or play with me the rest of vacation. She told Nana I was a bad influence on them, confirming what Nana knew already.

Nana says that we will be lucky if Mrs. Haggerty doesn't have a stroke, and that she probably won't ever speak to her again. Which of course she won't anyway, if she has the stroke. Can I go to jail for causing a stroke?

The very worst, worst part of what happened is, my big mystery is unsolved.

I want to go home and sit in the house near the air conditioner and read something that is not ND. I've heard the Hardy Boys books are better anyway.

Yours truly,
Maggie

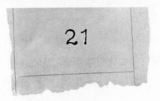

Holding the Bag

MAGGIE DID NOT come down for breakfast on Tuesday. Although she was hungry and figured you had to be a crazy person to miss one of Alma's meals, she didn't want to have to figure out the tangle of what to say to people.

It was a chilly, rainy morning. Maggie was learning that there were two types of rainy. There was the socked-in gray, cold, drizzly type that chilled your bones to watch it. And there was the stormy, booming, windy type that was frightening and exciting and you couldn't keep your eyes off the lake in case at any moment something would fall to destruction. It was the first kind. Which figured.

At first she ignored Alma's knock on her door, until Alma asked if she wanted a breakfast tray. That was Hannah Gruen-like, especially under the circumstances, and Maggie was grateful, so she said, "Yes, please."

Alma let Maggie balance the tray across her lap in bed, and even slapped her two pillows so they'd be puffy and upright behind her back. So far, really good. Then Alma pulled up the ladder-back chair that stood against the bedroom wall, tossing the clothes Maggie had piled there onto the foot of her bed, and sat next to her chummy-like.

Amazingly, Alma seemed to have forgotten the trauma at Haggerty's for the excitement over her morning list.

"I wanted you to see my list today, Miss Maggie. It's unusual, I will say, although I've had them written on everything from the back of a wedding invitation to a matchbox cover." She held out to Maggie a list that had been written with a heavy-lead pencil on the cardboard that comes from a package of stockings. Maggie giggled and Alma did too, and the fright of Alma's peering moon face was forgotten. It read

8:00 A.M. BREAKFAST: COFFEE AND ORANGE JUICE
BUTTERMILK PANCAKES AND SYRUP, SAUSAGE LINKS
10:00 A.M. PICNIC LUNCH FOR FRANK TO TAKE FISHING:
DEVILED HAM SANDWICHES WITH AN EXTRA ONE FOR THE
PROFESSOR.
DON'T FORGET THE OLIVES.
NOON: PICNIC LUNCH FOR MAGGIE ON THE BEACH:
DEVILED HAM SANDWICHES, GRAPES, AND CHOCOLATE BRIDGE
MIX.
GROCERY SHOPPING—AND GET YOURSELF AN ICE CREAM SODA
AT THUNDERBIRD'S

Maggie gasped on Alma's behalf, since this was something Nana might say to Maggie, but not to Alma

"Oh, and it gets better!"

6:00 P.M. DINNER: TROUT—FRANK GUARANTEES IT—NEW
FISHING SPOT TODAY. WITH LEFTOVERS OR WHATEVER SOUNDS
GOOD TO YOU.

"What's so special about leftovers?" asked Maggie.

"No." Alma tapped her pen and re-read the words, "It's this part: 'or whatever sounds good to you.'"

"Those words are b-e-a-u-t-i-f-u-l! And I know exactly what sounds good to me." Alma had written out her own menu, using pen, not pencil:

CHEESE GRITS

CALICO BEANS

RAINBOW TROUT

CORNBREAD

PINEAPPLE POUND CAKE

At the bottom of her menu she added her signature, in ink, in rounded, letters.

ALMA

After breakfast in bed, Maggie dressed and came downstairs to face the music with her grandmother. Nana sat at the desk writing on her monogrammed stationery. She greeted Maggie distractedly, so Maggie could not decipher between mad and distracted. Each time Maggie passed by her, Nana was staring at something, or nothing, through the rain. Wondering who Nana was writing to, Maggie took a quick, focused glance that showed her "Dearest Adele . . ."

This was not good.

Maggie sat at the dining room table playing Solitaire when, mid-morning, Mrs. Gerrard braved the rain in a slicker and hood to walk across the backyards to Kawuneeche. She climbed the stairs to the back porch, and stood with rain dripping off her just inside the back porch door. Alma was working at the sink and went out to the porch to greet her.

Quiet as a cumquat (Maggie's favorite word), Maggie took up her station against the closed swinging door to the kitchen. Watching through the crack, Maggie saw Mrs. Gerrard draw her hand from under her slicker and hand Alma a fringed leather purse and a fox

169

collar of the type where the fox's head bites his own tail. Mrs. Gerrard held up the fox by the tail, as if it would bite her if she gave it a chance. Alma laughed until she realized that Mrs. Gerrard wasn't.

"I found these in Bebo's possession last night. They must belong to Louise Haggerty, and I'm just mortified. I don't know what to say. How could they—? I trust that Maggie will see that they're returned, and that she makes it clear that she was the ring-leader."

"Thank you, Mrs. Gerrard. I'll give them to Maggie."

After Mrs. Gerrard left, Maggie remained at her post and watched Alma play with the fox head. She made it talk like a puppet; then she pulled out her rabbit's foot, and the fox chased it across the table. Maggie kept a tight rein on her desire to go play with the fox too, because there was more.

Alma clipped the fox collar around her neck and studied the leather bag.

The leather was a light brown calf's skin, soft and pliable, with leather drawstring handles and fringe across the center and bottom of the bag. Alma pulled open the puckered rim and dumped the contents onto the table, spread them out, and examined them one by one.

A used handkerchief

A crushed pack of cigarettes

One piece of pink saltwater taffy (Maggie liked that flavor, but it must be petrified)

A compact with a mirror in its lid, holding powder and a used powder puff

Red lipstick worn straight across instead of slanted

A comb

A piece of paper that looked like a shopping list

A ticket stub

Three sticks of Juicy Fruit gum, which must be board-brittle.

Alma unwrapped and sucked on one of the gum sticks, but eventually she spit it out into the used handkerchief. She gathered up the gum wrapper, the other sticks of gum, the taffy, the grocery list, and the handkerchief and took them to the back porch garbage can. Then she returned the other items to the leather-fringed bag, except for the ticket stub, which she slipped into her apron pocket.

Maggie quickly resumed her game of Solitaire in the dining room, since Alma was on her way to deliver the fox and bag to Nana, who was still sitting at the desk. Nana looked at Alma questioningly, then held her forehead in her hands as Alma explained it to her. She accepted the bag and fox from Alma, with no reply, and then Alma handed Nana that ticket stub from her pocket. They turned it over and discussed it quietly, then Nana looked around to see Maggie watching from the doorway, figuring she'd better just get it over with.

"Come here, Maggie," Nana said, turning in her chair to face the girl.

"Are you quite satisfied?" she asked.

What could she say? She had certainly not intended to hurt Nana, who was the one who had caught trouble the most.

"I didn't know about the bag, Nana, or the fox. I promise."

"But you were under Mrs. Haggerty's bed?" Nana' cheeks scrunched up disbelievingly. She was calm. Maggie had to give her that.

"I wanted to solve the mystery—if there was one. I'll stop now, Nana. I'm sorry that I made your friend so mad at you, and I hope she isn't sick. Maybe I do read too many Nancy Drew's." Maggie's cheeks felt hot.

"Unfortunately Louise hasn't seen the last of us this summer. We'll have to return this."

"Can we do it on our way out of town?"

"No, Maggie, let's get it over with this afternoon."

The rain spent itself before noon, but Maggie couldn't take her lunch to the dock, because Jamie and Bebo were picnicking on their beach right there within view. But when Nana went to the post office, Maggie came down to the kitchen to eat her sandwich and pick through the bridge mix with Alma.

It was nearly two o'clock when Nana returned from town in the car. Maggie heard the drone of an outboard motor coming toward their dock, and looked out to see that the lanky, pimple-faced boy who pumped boat gas at the marina was returning the repaired outboard.

Nana came to the porch, watched the boy park the boat, and put her hand on Maggie's shoulder. "Let me change my clothes, and then we'll go to Mrs. Haggerty's in the boat." Nana's hand felt cold on Maggie's shoulder. When Maggie looked up, Nana was staring out at the lake.

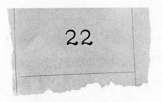

Released

WHEN NANA SAID it was time to go, Maggie pushed open the porch door, holding the ridiculous fox and the bag. Nana called her back, suggesting she might need her fringed leather jacket.

"My life jacket will keep me warm enough, Nana," Maggie shrugged off the idea. But Nana brought it out with her and handed it to Maggie, so she had to either carry it or put it on.

Nana stooped gracefully and stepped onto the middle seat of the small craft, indicating that Maggie was to drive, which pleased her, but also made her nervous, because she would have to watch her boating P's and Q's. Nana faced forward out-lake, her head swathed in a floppy hat and sunglasses. This registered a dangerously low reading on Maggie's Nana-O-Meter, because it was to read her.

Clouds hovered over the water, although above the clouds the mountain peaks gleamed against the blue sky. Maggie thought of Alma's root beer floats with their layers of dark soda pop, then frothy soda and cream, and at the top round peaks of ice cream peering above the glass rims. Maggie found it hard to remain somber when the lake and mountains looked like root beer floats, even though she couldn't identify anything to be light-hearted about.

At the Haggerty cottage, Nana knocked on the screen door. "Uoo Hoo," she called.

Coralee's face looked positively poka-dotted through the screen door.

"Is Louise available?" Nana asked.

The corners of Coralee's mouth slid down as she considered.

"Just a moment and I'll see. Why don't you go ahead and take a seat on the porch."

Nana brushed at a chair cushion and sat down. She removed her sun hat and her dark glasses, and Maggie detected a light in her grandmother's green eyes when she gazed at Maggie.

"Are you all right, Maggie?" Nana asked.

First there was the root beer float view, and now Nana's warming eyes. Maggie's muscles relaxed and she dangled the leather bag by its strings. She dared to point foxy's mouth toward Nana. "Ruff," she made it bark.

Nana half-laughed, swallowing it when Coralee reappeared at the screened door.

"Come on in, Mrs. Hamilton. Maggie can wait on the porch."

"Then Maggie and I will both wait on the porch to talk with Louise," Nana replied.

Coralee disappeared again.

"What is it, Jane?" Louise appeared at the door.

"Can we talk, please? Maggie has some things to return to you."

Mrs. Haggerty wore slacks and a red wool jacket with a bright Indian design on the back. She trusted her cane to help her onto the porch, then sat down and positioned it alongside her leg. She scowled when she caught sight of her fox wrap and fringed leather bag.

"What on earth is wrong with this girl?" Mrs. Haggerty asked Nana, as if Maggie was merely a statue upon which the items were draped. "What was she doing in my bedroom and my clothes closet?"

Mrs. Haggerty took her cane and reached forward with it, as if she was going to retrieve the fox and the bag with the gold tip.

Nana batted the cane away. Her face set into its wrinkles and the light left her eyes.

Maggie feared she had an old lady rumble on her hands. "I'm sorry, Mrs. Haggerty," Maggie said quickly. "I know we got carried away. But I really wanted to find your squash blossom necklace for you. I doubt that your daughter-in-law stole it." Maggie handed the items across to the old woman, but as she did, Nana intercepted the fringed leather bag.

"But-I-never-asked-you-to," Mrs. Haggerty spit out her words slowly. "You need to learn to mind your own business, missy!" Her head shook with a mild palsy, and the effect was like a continuous nodding for emphasis.

"In fact, you didn't want her to find it—or rather find out about it—did you Louise?" Nana asked, as she drew open the handles of the bag. "Let's see if Maggie is returning all your belongings."

Louise reached to Nana's lap and grabbed at the bag. "What on earth are you doing, Jane? Give me my bag right now. I can tell what should be in it."

Deftly, Nana jiggled the contents out onto the end table by her elbow and spread them out. "Here, maybe you'd like a cigarette, Louise," Nana asked, opening the pack on the table and tapping it against her index finger so that three cigarettes slid part way out.

"Why, Jane Hamilton. I never!"

"You know your necklace isn't missing, don't you, Louise?" Nana asked.

She put down the cigarettes and picked up the ticket stub. On one side it read:

MILLER'S INDIAN VILLAGE
PAWN ITEM NO. 602
LOUISE HAGGERTY
FOR SALE: JULY 10, 1946

And on the other side,

TRADITIONAL NAVAJO SQUASH BLOSSOM NECKLACE, CIRCA 1931

"It is none of your business—and certainly none of your granddaughter's business—what I choose to do with my property."

"Of course it isn't," said Nana, "but you didn't have to lead the girl on."

"But you asked me to lead her on," Louise sputtered.

"So why didn't you tell me the truth, and save us all this time and confusion? Maggie worried about your necklace her whole vacation."

"At first I had forgotten that I took it to Miller's last summer. And then when I remembered it, it didn't seem like anybody's business, like I said. And the more I thought about that daughter-in-law of mine, she would have stolen it if she could." Mrs. Haggerty tried to be emphatic, but her chin still jiggled up and down.

"I guess it wasn't my business, Mrs. Haggerty," said Maggie. "But at first, you really did seem upset. And if it had been stolen—well, those necklaces are so beautiful. You should see what one looks like on Alma."

Mrs. Haggerty looked like she'd eaten something sour and sounded like it too when she croaked, "On who?"

But Nana quickly smoothed things by changing the subject and saying now that the matter was settled, she hoped Mrs. Haggerty would come to bridge this week before we left for Kansas.

As they left Mrs. Haggerty's cabin, Maggie turned back toward her, standing with her cane in the doorway, to say, "I hope you at least received lots of money for your necklace, Mrs. Haggerty."

"Shhh!" Nana breathed—quick, like an exclamation point. "Leave it alone, Maggie." She steered Maggie's elbow toward the outboard.

* * *

On the way home, Nana turned around to face Maggie in the outboard.

"Maggie," she said gently, "I'm afraid the mystery of the missing squash blossom necklace was beneath your sleuthing abilities. I want you to know that I admire you for taking the high road. And I apologize for interfering." The light was back in Nana's green eyes.

The day had gone sunny, with a brisk east wind, and Maggie was having difficulty keeping the boat on course, pushing and pulling on the motor arm to keep it heading straight. She hoped that Nana thought the water now flooding her eyes was from the wind in her face. Nancy Drew would have remembered to wear sunglasses.

"I guess I pressed too hard," said Maggie, sniffling. "I'm sorry that I upset her."

"Some people don't want their mysteries solved, Maggie," said Nana. "They grow comfortable with them, and the truth takes them to a place they don't want to go. And then there are other mysteries that are not meant to be solved at all. The wondering is part of being human."

"Like about my daddy," Maggie said, wiping her nose on the back of her hand.

Nana squirmed on the metal boat seat. "What about your daddy?"

"He has bad dreams, Nana. He yells in the night and wakes up crying. But he won't tell me what he dreams about. I just want him to be all right. I don't know how to help him."

Maggie gave in to big blubbering, sloppy cries, and released pent-up sobs. Nana joined Maggie on the outboard's backseat and took the motor handle from her. She pulled some tissues from her sweater pocket and handed them to Maggie, who sobbed and sobbed, knowing that the sounds were covered by the engine's droning. Finally, Nana shifted the handle to her left hand, wrapped her right arm around Maggie, and held her tight as the outboard headed home.

23

Fish Fry

MAGGIE SAT ON the back stoop drinking a root beer and shelling peanuts, feeding some to herself and some to the two chipmunks scampering around the woodpile. On the back porch, Alma fanned herself with a folded newspaper from the trash bin, cooling and evaporating the rivulets of sweat on her face, when Grandpa and the Professor pulled in from their final day of fishing.

The two men pushed themselves out of the car, bellies bulging forward, arching their lower backs. Then they took loaded creels from the trunk of the car and handed them to Alma, who had been watching for them to arrive so she could marinate the trout and get them into the neighbor's smoker. The men patted each other on the back, obviously pleased with their contribution to the end-of-summer fish fry.

The grand fish fry would cap off the season, since most of the fishermen would be returning home to Kansas or Oklahoma or Texas or Denver in the next few days. Each of the maids or women would contribute dishes, and the meal would be served on card tables placed end-to-end on the Kawuneeche porch. The neighbor and bridge club families were all invited, including Mrs. Haggerty, who had not yet RSVPed.

Once Alma had delivered the trout to Francine, the maid next door, she sat down at the kitchen table with a Coke and looked again at the list for the day, written on a postcard from Bald Pate Inn in Estes. Nana had chosen dishes for the potluck menu that included some of Alma's crowning glories: Cheese Grits, Calico Beans, Fried Cornbread, and Pineapple Pound Cake, and as Alma held that Bald Pate card a hearty laugh rumbled from her stomach and filled the kitchen. "Yes!" Alma declared. "Yes. yes," over and over. Maggie joined her in the kitchen to be infected with her happiness. Alma told her that she could help with the preparations, but that she would have a signal. If the swinging door to the kitchen was open, Maggie could come in. If it was closed, she was not to enter, listen, or peek. Alma would be needing a little privacy and breathing room to sufficiently invoke her magic.

When she was ready to assemble her Pineapple Pound Cake, Alma opened the swinging door, knowing that Maggie loved to lick the bowl. Later Maggie returned to the kitchen when the oven timer chimed, and Alma carefully opened the oven door of the wood stove, so that the two of them could peer into its fragrant black interior. A bean pot bubbled with baby limas, pork and beans, cut green beans, and red kidney beans in an oozing sweet brown sugar sauce. A honey-colored crust covered cheese grits in a soufflé dish. The Pineapple Pound Cake was pooched up in the center and lightly golden.

Alma let Maggie poise a toothpick over the cake, to poke it and see if the toothpick came out clean.

"Do it real still, Miss Maggie," she said. "The sides of the cake aren't yet pullin' away from the pan, so it probably needs a few more minutes. Even footsteps could make it go cranky and fall."

Just then Uncle Max punched open the swinging door, ignorant of Alma's signals. "Alma, where's my plaid western shirt? Can't find it anywhere!" he bellowed, stomping into their hallowed kitchen. Maggie dropped the toothpick to fend for itself in the spongy dough, and Alma slammed the oven door in fright.

"That smells divine, by the way. What is it?"

Alma made a bee-line for the back porch to fetch another newspaper to fan her face, and Maggie glared at Uncle Max with her hands on her hips. Uncle Max had a shiny red pimple on the end of his nose that made him look harmless, an irritant rather than a threat. He scratched his cowlick, turned around, and left.

Later, after Alma took the cake out of the oven, none the worse for the experience except for gaining a little wood pulp from the toothpick, Alma set the tables with Maggie's help, until Nana called Maggie upstairs to change into her squaw skirt and blouse.

It didn't seem right to Maggie that she should sit at the far end of the room at the Kiddie Table with Jamie and Bebo, since she had helped set the train-car-long dining table with red and white gingham tablecloths, red candles set in the Mexican wrought-iron candleholders, and Nana's cobalt blue Fiestaware. But at least, she figured, she was the host for the kids' table. And she interpreted the white napkin that Mrs. Gerrard flipped open and spread across her lap as a flag of truce: she obviously didn't believe Maggie's influence to be harmful to her children, because there they were, their hands grabbing for pieces of warm cornbread, at Maggie's table.

Once the maids had passed around all the serving dishes and their plates were loaded, Maggie demonstrated to her chums the way to eat trout that the Professor was also demonstrating (and had previously demonstrated to Maggie at one of many dinners at the cabin), further up the train. You remove the dorsal fin at the back of the trout, and the head of course, and then you hold it up and chomp down the spine like it was corn on the cob. Jamie took tiny, tentative pecks at her trout's skinny back. Bebo attacked his with all the teeth he could muster, left plenty of tender morsels on his plate with the skeleton, and asked for a second trout.

Alma bent over the long table, pouring water and replenishing dishes. She wore her best for-company black taffeta uniform, her starched white apron, and her white cotton crown. Although two other maids served with her, Alma was the queen. When Maggie looked up the table later, she was surprised to find Alma gone, because Alma's presence seemed to hover in the room, over their plates, the forkfuls of tender pink trout meat; the soft, grainy cheese grits; and the spicy/sweet Calico Beans.

As usual, Maggie the Sleuth attended to conversations around her. The voices up the table mingled, then a voice surfaced. Then a silence and conversations split in pairs.

"—and you've given the readers fresh material, Janie. I've very proud of the job you've done," Grandpa said. Nana squirmed on her chair and showed her dimples.

"I have received some letters about my last column that were less than complimentary."

"But it hasn't soured you, has it Janie?"

"No, I think I'm finding my voice," Nana said, looking satisfied and handsome, even with a big nose.

"Good meeting with the Bureau, Frank," said the Professor, with a mouthful of cornbread.

"Uphill climb. I know you'll keep me posted," said Grandpa.

Then laughter.

The fishermen each told a favorite story about a conquest, or near-conquest, on the streams. "When I wade into those chilly waters," Grandpa's voice rose, "and I fling a Red Quill fly to tickle the water above where I suspect is a hungry rainbow or brown, the rest of the world falls away. It's just me and the fish and the river. And peace." Glasses were raised toward him and clinked in a toast.

"Here, here."

"That's right."

"That's it."

"What was it like when you took back the fox and the bag?" Bebo asked Maggie, louder than she wished.

"Did Old Lady Haggerty really pawn the necklace?" Jamie asked. Then she curled her fingers into stiff claws and raised them, imitating her, "Help! Help! Help!"

"Shhhhh," Maggie said, ducking her head as some of the adults turned their heads to listen.

"What do you mean, 'Shhhh'? You're the one who scared her to death. The old witch! Got us into plenty of trouble, I'll tell you that."

Maggie thought of Mrs. Haggerty in her house across the lake, with no company but Coralee, while at Kawuneeche they dined in style. "Leave her be, Jamie. I should of cared more about her, used a little . . . finesse."

"Oh, brother! Now will you give up the Nancy Drew act?" Jamie asked.

Maggie glanced up the long table to see Nana watching her, listening, taking in their conversation while she took delicate bites. And Nana gave Maggie the new eye. Not a turtle eye, but a winked eye. And more! Nana picked up her wine glass and held it her way. A toast.

"Are you kidding? After finding and solving my first mystery? I'm not perfect, but I bet I'm younger than ND was when she started," Maggie said. Jamie sighed and Bebo kept eating trout. Maggie took the high road and did not mention the handicap of half-hearted accomplices.

What about the reward? As Alma brought in slices of her Pineapple Pound Cake, each soaking up a drizzle of confectioner's sugar and pineapple juice, Maggie looked out the screens at the gloaming. Lights twinkled in cabins across the lake, a reminder of a loose summer community: I'm here, I'm here . . . they seemed to say. Even, maybe, people were eating dinner in the cabin where her mother's old boyfriend had lived. And Maggie thought how wonderful her summer had been after all. You never knew how things would work out when you started.

"Ouch!" Nana pulled a sliver of broken toothpick out of her mouth. She searched for Alma, but she wasn't in the room. So she looked toward Maggie with her eyebrows furrowed, but Maggie became occupied moving food on her plate with her fork.

Toward the end of the meal, Uncle Max appeared with his camera. He took a picture down the long, dish-strewn table. Then he set up his own little picture booth in front of the fireplace and took everyone's picture: The bridge ladies (except Mrs. Haggerty). Nana and Grandpa with their arms comfortably around each other. Grandpa and the Professor. The Professor and Maggie (at his request). Maggie between Nana and Grandpa. Maggie, Jamie, and Bebo (Maggie had to pester them for this one). And he even pushed open the kitchen door and snapped some surprise shots of Alma, Francine, and Luellen. Alma wanted one of herself in front of the wood stove, with her arms folded, and her head high. Dr. Gerrard snapped a photo of Uncle Max, Jeffry Wyatt, and Susan and Teensy from next door. Then the photo session dissolved into photos of just Teensy and Susan in every pose Uncle Max could persuade of them. Maggie tried to get into one, but Uncle Max firmly denied her.

Closings

Dear Diary Friday, August 29, 1947

One thing that's different about cabins than about the house where you always live is that you have to open and close them, so there's the hub-bub over first things and last things. We've been busy this week getting things closed up.

After the big fish fry, Uncle Max got right up for breakfast and spent most of the morning in the darkroom. He gave us each copies of our photographs. I noticed that the ones of the girls next door were bigger than the rest of them. It didn't take Uncle Max long at all after that to pack his car and head for Kansas. He said he had college friends to see along the way. While he packed his record albums in a box, I told him I was really sorry, but if he loved the "The Whiffenpoof Song," he'd be needing a new one. He looked at me funny, but that's all I said, to keep Alma out of it. As soon as Alma got her photographs, she scurried over next door to show Francine.

Grandpa and Nana look handsome in theirs. They both have suntans and Nana's hair is swooped back nicely, and she's letting her dimples show. I'm the girl in the glasses with the fancy barrette and the squaw skirt, looking pretty much like usual in pictures, except I do look taller.

Nana had to write her last column, pretty much back to the who came to the fish fry, and how many trout they caught, and that they were going to Estes Park, so that Grandpa (the rightful editor) could attend a big meeting about cleaning up the lake, a project that should keep lots of people busy for a long time. But the best part was her last paragraph where she wrote, and I quote, "The highlight of my summer was the presence of our granddaughter Maggie, a sleuth of exceptional ability for her eleven years. She solved the mystery of the missing squash blossom necklace, and helped me in my search for a good vacation." That is better than the widow and orphan reward, if you ask me.

Yesterday, Nana and Grandpa went to the big Bureau of Wreck-the-Nation meeting (that's what Nana calls it—haha) in Estes Park, leaving Alma and me to our own devices, but of course Alma had a list to do. When Alma finished her morning chores, we set out for town.

First we stopped in at the mayor's café, because I thought he should have a copy of Nana's column that she wrote about the Big Back-Up, and one of the photographs that Uncle Max took of him. Nana had received a whole pile of copies of the column from friends at home, so I didn't think she'd mind if I took one to the mayor. He probably didn't think she was really a journalist, but I guess she is, and he'd better get serious about the sewage clean-up.

While Alma went into the post office to arrange to get the mail forwarded back home, I walked down to the stable. Jamie was there all right, in her riding get-up. She leaned against the corral watching a wrangler practice rope tricks. She motioned me to come close to her and whispered, with her hand covering the sound waves from her mouth to my ear, "He's crazy about me."

I told her I doubted it. She said that I might have solved the squash blossom necklace mystery, but I didn't know anything about boys. We said we'd see each other next summer, but I didn't mention being pen pals, and neither did she.

When we met back up, Alma had happy tears because she had hit the jackpot in General Delivery. Here she'd been stewing all month because she hadn't gotten a letter from her husband Baxter. But when she finally didn't just check Nana and Grandpa's mailbox, but asked in General Delivery if there was any mail for Alma Carter, they brought her two letters—one stale one, and one fresh one. Even though she was carrying her pocketbook, she tucked them into her bosom to read when we got home.

From the PO we walked up the street to Thunderbird's. In my coin purse I had money Nana gave us to each buy a souvenir. First we sat on stools at the soda counter and drank ice cream sodas: mine cherry and hers chocolate. Alma needed two stools if you ask me, but she heaved up onto one and said she could manage. I pulled out the money and put it on the counter and said, "Here is the reward for solving the mystery of the missing squash blossom necklace. How shall we spend it, Hannah?" and I smiled at her, so she knew I was kidding. The soda jerk stopped fizzing the soda he was working on and watched us, so I smiled at him too.

Then we walked to the jewelry counter and found the same old maid schoolteacher saleslady as before, and asked her to bring out more samples than we really needed to make our decisions. I chose a ring with many colored stones in the shape of a sun, because it looked like a big smiling face. And what did Alma choose but a silver bracelet with one of those upside-down horseshoe fertility symbols. This could make me very nervous if I think about it. It's one thing to have my mother out of commission with a baby; but what would we do without Alma?

Nana and Grandpa got home from Estes Park after I'd gone to bed last night, but this morning Nana told me all about it.

Grandpa's meeting went pretty well, but he said that it would be the first of many, many, more of them, so he was glad to be going back to Kansas.

While Grandpa was at the meeting, Nana ate lunch at the Baldpate Inn and left a key to Kawuneeche in their Key Room. Next time I want her to take me with her to see this place with thousands of keys dangling from the ceiling. Just think of the mysteries that wait behind some of those doors!

Nana stopped by Miller's Indian Village and made a point of looking at their pawned jewelry. A squash blossom necklace sat there in the case that she was sure was Mrs. Haggerty's, meaning that it hadn't even sold yet. But Nana said she didn't ask the clerk to verify if Mrs. Haggerty was the owner, because this felt mean-spirited.

Today we packed and cleaned. Grandpa and the boat service man got the boats up on chains in the boathouse, with wooden cribbings under them in case a chain broke and they fell down. The Professor came over to help Grandpa oil his fishing line, draping it across the trees, and to put his gear away. They stood down at the car for a long time "kicking the tires," as Nana calls it when men lean against cars and talk. Then they slapped each other on the shoulders, and the Professor left.

Alma and I aren't looking forward to the long, hot ride in the back of the Grey Gazelle. Well, at least I'm not. Alma says she's not, but she was sure packed early. She says Nana's promised her a week's vacation.

So tomorrow we head back to Kansas. I'll get to go to the fair with Daddy, and I will do my best with my mother. Maybe it will help that now I know she had a summer romance.

Sincerely,
Maggie

Early Start

NANA WOKE MAGGIE at 5:00 a.m. on Saturday. It was still dark. Maggie's stomach felt jumpy from the leaving and the going home and the fact that it didn't feel right to be up at that hour. They had to eat breakfast quickly—cold cereal and toast, the last of the milk and the last of the orange juice—so Alma could finish getting the kitchen emptied of food and buttoned up.

Maggie went back to her room to do her final things. Her suitcase lay open on her chair. She took the silver bead from her drawer, still wrapped in her bandana, and tucked it into the corner of her suitcase. Then she stored her locked diary and its tiny key in the satin compartment on her suitcase lid.

"Maggie, we're ready to leave," Nana called from the first floor. "Bring your suitcase and let's go."

Then Maggie placed her two Nancy Drew mysteries on top of her folded pajamas, and closed her suitcase.

Finally, she took her fringed leather jacket, which she had fetched from the peg on the front porch, put it on a hanger, and held it up to admire. She cleaned the pockets of used tissues, band-aid wrappers, and a nickel she'd found in the road. Then she buttoned the buttons.

It seemed to belong here, where her great-grandmother had worn it, and where she found her first mystery.

"Maggie! Come on. We're going to the car," Grandpa called from the bottom of the stairs.

Then she hung the jacket in her closet, on the lower rod, and when she did, she couldn't help but see it. Her clothes must have hidden it, but why didn't she see it when she first hung them up? In the back wall of her closet was a big-as-you-please, definite secret compartment. Extending from the floor, a piece of wood a couple of feet square was cut out of the wall and anchored back in by three turnable wooden tabs. She turned the tabs, but the board still stuck, wedged in by the baseboard along the bottom of the closet wall. She pried at the board with her stubby fingernails, but couldn't get them into the cracks to pull the board away. Frantically, Maggie yanked open her top dresser drawer to look for a nail file or screw driver— something thin and sharp, but she'd left the drawer bare.

"Maggie, we're waiting!" Suddenly Nana stood in the bedroom. "What are you doing?"

"Nana, it's a real secret compartment," Maggie's face felt hot. "Did you know it was here?"

Nana squatted to examine it. "No, I had no idea."

"Oh! What's in it? If you'll just help me. Pull on this side—"

Nana wedged her polished nails into the crevices and tried to pull, but the board stuck. "It must have been here a long time, Maggie. I can't seem to budge it."

Suddenly Maggie put her hands squarely onto the center of the panel, and then turned each of the three wooden tabs back into place. She hung the fringed coat in front of the secret compartment, shut her closet door, closed her suitcase, and carried it out into the hall while Nana sat on the bed and watched. Then Maggie leaned back in the doorway. "Come on, Nana," she said, winking. "Next year."

Alma's Recipes

Arkansas Hot Pepper Pecans

INGREDIENTS

¼ cup butter

2 cups pecan halves

4 tsp. soy sauce

1 tsp. salt

12 dashes Tabasco sauce

METHOD

Melt butter in baking pan. Spread pecans evenly in pan and bake at 300° for 30 minutes. Combine soy sauce, salt and Tabasco sauce and toss with pecans. Spread on paper towels to cool.

Mushroom Rollups

INGREDIENTS

½ cup butter
1 cup flour
½ tsp. salt
4 oz. small-curd cottage cheese
12 oz. fresh mushrooms, chopped
2 T. butter
Salt and pepper to taste
Onion salt to taste
3 T. sesame seeds or caraway seeds
2 T. butter, melted
1 egg, beaten
Dash onion salt

METHOD

Cut ½ cup butter into flour and salt until lumps are pea-sized. Stir in cottage cheese and press into ball. Refrigerate at least 2 hours. Sauté mushrooms briefly in 2 tablespoons butter. Season to taste with salt, pepper and onion salt. Set aside. Sprinkle floured board with seeds and roll dough to a 15" x 8" rectangle. Cut rectangle in half, lengthwise, and spread each piece with melted butter. Spread half of mushroom filling on each piece of dough.

Beginning with longest edge, roll up, jelly-roll fashion. Place rolls on cookie sheet and chill 1 hour.

When ready to bake, brush tops of rolls with egg and sprinkle lightly with onion salt. Cut into ½" slices; place slices on cookie sheet and bake at 400° for 15 minutes, or until golden. Makes 4 dozen.

Wolferman's Chocolate Drop Cookies

INGREDIENTS

Cookies:
¾ cup sugar
½ cup butter
¼ tsp. vanilla
¼ tsp. salt
¼ cup light corn syrup
2 eggs
4 oz. unsweetened chocolate, melted and cooled
½ cup milk
1-3/4 cup flour
1-1/2 tsp. baking powder
¼ cup pecans, chopped

Icing:
2 oz. unsweetened chocolate
2 T. butter
¼ cup milk
2 cup powdered sugar
1 tsp. vanilla
Dash salt

METHOD

Cream sugar, butter, vanilla, salt and corn syrup. Add eggs and chocolate. Add milk slowly, and stir in flour and baking powder. Add pecans. Drop by teaspoonsful on greased cookie sheet and bake at 325° for 10 minutes. Makes 2 dozen large cookies.

Prepare icing by melting chocolate and butter together. Heat milk and pour over powdered sugar, vanilla and salt. Add chocolate mixture to sugar mixture and mix. Spread on cooled cookies.

Monte Carlo Squares

INGREDIENTS
¾ cup butter
1/3 cup sugar
1/8 tsp. salt
2 egg yolks
1-1/2 cups flour
1 cup apricot preserves
2 egg whites
½ cup sugar
2 oz. almonds, sliced

METHOD
Mix butter, sugar, salt, egg yolks and flour. Pat into 9" x 9" buttered and floured pan. Bake for 20 to 25 minutes at 350°. Remove from oven and spread with apricot preserves. Beat egg whites with sugar until stiff and spread over apricot preserves. Sprinkle with almonds and return to oven for 25 to 30 minutes. Cut into 16 squares. Cool before removing from pan.

Fresh Coconut Cake

INGREDIENTS
1 cup butter
2 cups sugar
4 eggs, separated
1-1/2 tsp. vanilla
2-2/3 cups cake flour
1-1/2 tsp. baking powder
½ tsp. salt
1 coconut
½ cup liquid from coconut
½ cup milk

METHOD
Preheat oven to 350°. Cream the butter (do not use margarine) and sugar together until light. Separate the eggs, setting whites aside. Beat egg yolks into butter and sugar mixture, one at a time. Add vanilla.

Sift the cake flour before measuring. Resift measured flour with baking powder and salt. Pierce the coconut and strain ½ cup of the liquid into a measuring cup. Combine the coconut liquid and the milk in a small bowl.

Add the sifted dry ingredients to the butter and sugar mixture in three parts, alternating with the coconut liquid and milk mixture. Beat well after each addition.

Beat the egg whites until stiff and fold into the batter. Pour into three greased 9-inch cake pans and bake at 250° for 30 minutes. Remove from pans before completely cool.

Frosting

INGREDIENTS
 1-½ cups sugar
 2 egg whites
 5 tablespoons water
 Pinch of cream of tartar
 6 large marshmallows
 1 tsp. vanilla
 2 cups freshly grated coconut

METHOD
Place all ingredients except vanilla and coconut in the top of a double boiler set over simmering water. Cook for about seven minutes, beating constantly with an electric hand mixer at high speed. The frosting should be stiff and glossy. Remove from heat and stir in vanilla

When cool, spread on cake. Grate coconut meat and sprinkle between each layer and on top and sides of cake.

Coconut cake is a traditional Easter dessert in the South.

Vegetable Aspic Salad

INGREDIENTS

   1 box Knox's gelatin soaked in a little cold water
   ½ pint boiling water
   ½ pint iced water
   ½ cup sugar
   1 cup vinegar
   1 small can pimentos
   3 green peppers, chopped fine
   2 bunches celery, all chopped fine
   2 cups cabbage, cut fine with slaw cutter

METHOD

Mix all together and pour in moulds.

CHEESE GRITS

INGREDIENTS

1-1/2 cups grits
6 cups water
1 lb. New York sharp cheese, grated
¾ cup butter
3 eggs, beaten
1 T. seasoned salt
1 tsp. paprika
2 tsp. salt
Several drops Tabasco sauce

METHOD

Cook grits in 6 cups water according to package directions. While still warm, add remaining ingredients. (May be prepared ahead to this point.) Bake in 2-1/2 quart buttered soufflé dish for 1 to 1-1/2 hours at 350°. Serves 12.

Calico Beans

INGREDIENTS

½ pound bacon
1 onion, chopped
10 oz. package frozen baby lima beans
16 oz. can pork and beans, undrained
16 oz. can cut green beans, drained
16 oz. can red kidney beans, drained
½ cup ketchup
½ cup brown sugar
¼ cup wine (or 2 T. vinegar)
1 T. prepared mustard
½ tsp. salt

METHOD

Fry bacon. Drain and crumble. Sauté onion in 2 tablespoons of bacon grease until golden. Cook limas according to package directions. Drain and combine all ingredients. Bake in 2-qt. casserole or bean pot at 300° for 1 to 2 hours. Serves 12. (To reheat, add additional wine.)

Rainbow Trout

INGREDIENTS

For one good-sized trout

¼ cup butter or bacon grease

½ cup cornmeal

½ teaspoon each salt and pepper

½ teaspoon cayenne pepper

METHOD

Rinse the cleaned trout under cold running water and then pat dry. Mix together the cornmeal, salt, pepper, and cayenne pepper in a pan and coat both sides of the trout.

Heat the butter in a skillet large enough to hold the trout. When the butter is melted, place the coated trout, flesh side down, in the skillet. Fry 4-5 minutes, then turn and fry 4-5 minutes, or until the flesh is golden brown and flaky.

To test for doneness, stick a fork into the thickest part of the trout. If it is perfectly cooked it is nearly opaque, should be moist, and will flake easily with a fork.

Fried Cornbread

INGREDIENTS

Bacon drippings

2 cups white corn meal

½ cup flour

1 tsp. salt

1 tsp. sugar

2-1/2 tsp. baking powder

1 egg, beaten

4 T. melted butter

1 T. melted vegetable shortening

2 cups milk

METHOD

Preheat oven to 400°. Grease a cast iron skillet with bacon drippings and place in the oven.

Sift the corn meal, flour, salt, sugar and baking powder together into a mixing bowl. Add the beaten egg, melted butter and melted shortening. Stir in the milk and mix well. Pour the mixture into the piping hot skillet and bake at 400° for 45 minutes, or until lightly browned on top. Serve immediately with butter.

PINEAPPLE POUND CAKE

INGREDIENTS
- 1-½ cups butter
- 8-1/2 cups sifted powdered sugar, divided
- 6 eggs
- 1 tsp. lemon juice
- 1 tsp. vanilla
- 3-½ cups sifted flour
- 2-½ cups crushed pineapple
- ½ cup (reserved) pineapple juice

METHOD

Preheat oven to 325°. In a large mixing bowl, cream the butter and 6-1/2 cups of the powdered sugar together. Add the eggs one at a time, beating well. Stir in the lemon juice and vanilla. Add the sifted flour all at once and beat well with a wooden spoon.

Drain the crushed pineapple in a colander for at least one hour, occasionally tossing with a fork. Reserve the juice for the glaze. Stir the pineapple into the batter.

Pour the mixture into a greased tube pan and bake at 325° for 1-1/2 hours, or until a toothpick inserted in the cake comes out clean. When the cake has almost cooled, turn out of the pan and glaze.

To glaze the cake, combine ½ cup of the pineapple juice with the remaining two cups of powdered sugar. Blend well and spoon over the warm cake.

Acknowledgments

TURQUOISE SUMMER WAS written over many summers. At one point my husband said, "You don't want to finish this, do you?" And indeed I didn't, because I enjoyed it so much. But I have. And countless people have helped me with encouragement and with nuggets of information. My gratitude especially goes to these Grand Lake neighbors, readers, editors, family, and generous friends:

Tim Thompson, Gay Shaffer, Jane Patience Kemp, Richard Mc-Queary, Barbara Thompson Bowes, Mac Ruske, Karen J. Parks, Lydia Hunter, Peggy A. Ford, Canton O'Donnell, Annie O'Donnell, Mert Leeper, Wayne Lumpkin, Sara Guettel, Dr. John Stahl, Mary Leeper, Nancy Lavington, Cynthia Fry Wilson, Karen Fry Weisbrich, Leslie Franz, Jane Claes, Anne Kremmer Massey, Bonnie Sutherland, Sarah Sutherland, Caroline Riley, Linda Bruce, Robert Scott, Robert Howey, Mary Howey, The Book Doctors' Pitchapalooza, Eliza Cross, Mary Taylor Young, Annabelle Deline, Gordon Scheer, Marjorie Hooper, Dr. Michael Brooks, Raymond Osborne, Toni Miller, Dr. Joseph Metz, Jan Metz, Joanna Perkins, Kathy James Rinker, Elin Capps, Elisa Morgan, Terri Blaskovich, Marcia Ford, Judy Joss, Barbara Stuber, Vinitia Swonger, Patty Fahy, Steve DeBeer, Stephanie Bruno, Maria St. Louis-Sanchez, Patricia Wishart, Lighthouse Writers Workshop, Don Chubb, and David Chubb. Admiration to Alma Connelly Byrd, whom I never met, and to Andrew Lagerborg, for giving me courage.

To my wise and encouraging critique group friends The Wonderfuls—Kathleen Groom, Lindsey O'Connor, and Shelly Steig—you're the best!

Love to my husband Alex. Thanks for understanding, for making space and time, for buying me a laptop so I would pursue my dream, and for making sure that I got it done.

About the Author

MARY BETH LAGERBORG is an author of non-fiction and a personal historian who since children has spent summers in Grand Lake, Colorado. *Turquoise Summer* is her first novel.